SAM
and the
MOON QUEEN

Alison Cragin Herzig
and Jane Lawrence Mali

■ ■ ■ ■ ■ ■ ■ ■ ■ ■ ■ ■ ■ ■ ■ ■ ■ ■

SAM
and the
MOON QUEEN

Clarion Books ▪ New York

Acknowledgments

We wish to express our deep appreciation to Jill Herzig for her unsentimental editorial help when we needed it the most, and to the staff and students at the Walden Lincoln School.

Clarion Books
a Houghton Mifflin Company imprint
215 Park Avenue South, New York, NY 10003

Text copyright © 1990 by Alison Cragin Herzig
and Jane Lawrence Mali

Library of Congress Cataloging-in-Publication Data

Herzig, Alison Cragin.
    Sam and the moon queen / by Alison Cragin Herzig and Jane Lawrence
Mali.
       p. cm.
    Summary: Sympathetic to a homeless girl's plight, Sam tries to
help her find food for herself and medical aid for her dog.
    ISBN 0-395-53342-2
    [1. Homeless persons—Fiction.] I. Mali, Jane Lawrence.
II. Title.
PZ7.H432478Sam   1990
[Fic]—dc20   89-77664
                                           CIP
                                           AC

BP 10 9 8 7 6 5 4 3 2 1

For Elizabeth Isele,
friend, editor and
the first who said,
"Believe it."

SAM
and the
MOON QUEEN

"Help me with the bed," Mom said, "so we can eat."

"It isn't a bed," I said, but I picked up the end of the metal frame and folded the mattress into the sofa. Mom fit in the seat cushions. Now the room was back to being a living dining kitchen again. I stuffed Mom's pillow on top of the boxes in the closet. When I closed the door, an edge of pillowcase hung out like underwear from a suitcase.

I thought about our old place, with a kitchen we could sit in and a hall with real bedrooms off it.

"Is it hot or what?" Mom said. She moved the chairs and pulled the round table out from the corner.

Tommy would have a million small room jokes for this dump, I thought. They'd all be right on. You could stand in front of the sofa and practically touch every wall.

"What do you want for lunch?" Mom opened the

refrigerator door. She was wearing her black waitressing pants and the orange vest with the lace handkerchief exploding out of the pocket. She wore her uniform a lot of the time. She said it saved money on clothes. But still I hated that she had to go on the bus dressed like that.

"We've got snacks and sides, that's all Salvi had left over at closing time. Half a Diner Piggy Platter and some Chinese chicken wings. And I made some lemonade. I figured anything hot would kill us."

"Why can't we have spaghetti ever?" I said.

"We do," Mom said, "but the stuff from the diner is free."

"I'm not really hungry anyway."

"Sam, honey, a thirteen-year-old boy has to eat. How do you expect to grow if you live on Coca-Cola?"

"I eat," I said.

—"No, you don't. You mope. You've been moping for the past week, ever since we moved." She slapped plates on the table. "Now sit down and put something in your mouth."

I gave up and straddled a chair. "Is there any dessert?"

"Half a strawberry shortcake. Mona filched it for you. And take off that sweaty baseball cap."

"I can't," I said. "You gave me the worst haircut."

"Sorry." Mom picked up her glass of lemonade and rolled it across her forehead.

That was mean, I thought. It wasn't that bad a haircut, only a little too short. "At least it's even," I said. "Too short on both sides."

Mom smiled. "I wish I could take a bath in ice cubes."

I stared past her. The room looked out on nothing but walls with squares and squares of windows rising to a little puzzle piece of sky. In our old apartment on the north side I could see things from the windows. And when it was hot like this I used to go up on the roof with Tommy and Lou. It was great. There was a breeze up there. Tommy would smoke and we would spit over the rail and barricade the roof door and pretend no one could get us. But that was before Mom made us move.

"So what did you do this morning while I was asleep?"

This was our time to talk. Mom worked the night shift at the diner. So in the summer when I wasn't in school, she slept late.

"Nothing," I said.

"You must have done something," Mom said. "You just got home."

"Yeah, well, I was throwing a ball against the wall of that storage warehouse. The one down by the river?"

"Isn't it nice," Mom said, "being close to the river. You don't hear the trains anymore and it isn't so dirty and crowded."

"I liked our old neighborhood," I said.

"It's a lot safer here."

"Mom, the guy only took my bus pass. It was no big event. It's not like I got maimed or something."

"You were lucky," Mom said. "It could have been someone on drugs with all those dealers moving in."

"I wish I'd never told you. Then Mona would never have gotten you to move in here."

"Don't blame it on her. I was already looking for another apartment. Before she even found that bigger place."

"She sure needs a bigger place," I said. Mona was fat. Tommy had a million jokes for her, too.

"That reminds me," Mom said. "I need a new dream. The week's up."

Ever since Mona started working at the diner, Mom's been playing Lotto. Mona uses a system called dream betting. You look up a word from your dream to find out its number in this book called *The Three Wise Men.* The only problem is that Mom can never remember her dreams, so she has to use mine.

"I've got one, but you're not going to like it," I said. "It was Dad and Beans again."

Mom hesitated. Then she pulled *The Three Wise Men* out from under the sugar bowl.

"Okay, tell me."

"They were alive," I said, "so you weren't a waitress yet. And we went to a baseball game. Only it wasn't in a stadium, it was in the playground. And there were a lot of people on the jungle gym eating popcorn and speaking Spanish."

"Playground, baseball, Spanish . . ." Mom repeated. "Then what?"

"Nothing. Suddenly Dad and Beans disappeared. They got up and left before the end."

"That's death," Mom said.

I knew it. Mom always says that. She says that about 99 percent of the time. She always finds death in my dreams, somewhere. If I say night or tunnel or people shrinking, she jumps on it. I knew the number for death in her dream book by heart.

"Death never works," I said.

Mom sat there, quiet. I wished I'd kept my mouth shut. I mean Dad and Beans are on my mind, sometimes, but I wasn't that sad anymore. The hard part was to see Mom be sad.

"What about popcorn?" I said.

"Popcorn?"

"Yeah. Popcorn. We've never used that before."

"Okay," said Mom. "Look it up." She handed me the pamphlet. I flipped through the pages. You name it, there was a number for it. If you dreamed about someone named Arthur, there was one number to bet. But if you dreamed about Geraldine, there was a different number. There were numbers for everything. Acute indigestion, Buzzard, Dog. The number for Dog was 7-17-27. Marmalade, Pimples, Pyramid, I'd gone too far. I ran my finger back.

"It's here," I said. "6-31-4."

Mom wrote it on a paper napkin. "Hey, it looks lucky. Thanks, hon. Now I'd better get going or I'll be late. Put the food away for me, okay?"

"Okay." I always had to do that.

"And remember to double lock if you go out."

"Okay." She told me that every single time.

"And keep the chain on if you stay in."

"Okay!" She was always warning me.

"And call me at the diner."

"Okay. Okay!"

"And why don't you call Lou and see if he wants to come over and watch TV with you tonight."

"Maybe," I said. "Or maybe I'll call Tommy."

"Oh, Sam, not Tommy."

"You're always on me. He's one of my best friends."

"But he runs wild," Mom said. "Nobody cares what he does. You have a chance now to meet some nice new kids."

"That's great, Mom, really great," I said. "How?"

"You'll meet somebody. At the Boys' Club. You haven't even tried that yet. And then you can invite them home."

"Here?"

"Of course, here." Mom's voice rose. "You're not giving this place half a chance."

She was right. I wasn't. I couldn't help it. Just because I had a bed here didn't make it home.

"Aren't you going to be late?" I said. I checked Dad's old watch.

Just then the buzzer sounded.

"What's that? The doorbell?" Mom asked.

"No. It's from downstairs," I said.

"Oh, the intercom? I wonder who it is."

The buzzer rang again. Suddenly I had this great thought. It was Tommy and Lou, come to surprise me.

"Remember," Mom said, "never buzz anyone in without knowing who it is." She picked up the receiver. "Hello? Who? . . . Oh, Mona. Hold on. I'll let you in."

Mom hung up the receiver and turned to me. "It's Mona," she said, as though I were deaf.

I slumped back into my chair. I wasn't up for Mona. It was too hot. "What's she doing here?" I asked.

"I guess she was in her old neighborhood. We can go over to the diner together."

At least she wouldn't be here long, I thought.

Mom opened the door and stared out into the hall. I heard the elevator creaking upward.

"Hi," said Mom. "You're just in time for a quick glass of . . . hey, Mona. What's wrong?" She took a step back. "What's the matter?"

Mona filled the doorway and then she filled the living room. She was dressed just like Mom, but she was so big her orange vest looked ten sizes too small, as if she'd put on a little kid's life jacket. And she was carrying a suitcase. She dropped the suitcase and lowered herself onto the sofa.

"Skinny over, Flo," she said. "I've got to move back in."

2
....

For a moment Mom just stood there staring at the suitcase. Then she folded her arms across her chest. "Why?" she asked. "What's happened?"

"It's the landlord. He wants to sell the building, so he's trying to force all the tenants out. The guy I sublet the apartment from never told me."

"What do you mean, 'out'?" Mom asked.

"Out, like o-u-t, out," Mona said. "The landlord keeps turning off the electricity. No elevator. And no lights. Four floors I walked up this morning. In the dark."

She looked pinkish and wet and her red lipstick was melting up into her skin.

"Yesterday there were three goons in the hall." Mona sagged back and fanned herself with her hand.

"Goons?" I asked. "What did they look like?"

"They had tattoos," Mona said. "And baseball bats. It's scary. I can't stay there."

Three against one. It sounded bad.

"Oh, Mona," Mom said. "That's terrible."

"I know," Mona said. She stared at Mom. "But where else can I go?"

I didn't know, but she couldn't stay here, I thought. Her perfume seemed to be everywhere. It used up the air.

"Well," Mom said, "of course you're welcome. This is your apartment after all."

There were a million bad things about this place, but this was one thing I'd never thought of. I stood up and edged toward the hall to my room.

"I'm really sorry," Mona said.

"What are friends for." Mom glanced around the room. "Would you like a glass of lemonade? I made some fresh."

"Anything cold, Flo. And for God's sake turn up the air conditioner."

"You took it with you, remember?"

"Well, I can't breathe," Mona said.

"It's not that bad," I said. "Mom and I don't mind."

"Sam, honey, get this suitcase out of the way. Put it . . ." Mom looked around again, "in your room for the time being."

I didn't move. Mom dragged the suitcase over to me. "Please, honey," she said low.

At least I didn't have to carry it that far. Three steps past the bathroom and I was there. I put the suitcase down by my desk. There was my bed and my red rug and the chair that Dad had repainted black. But now there was Mona's suitcase. It took over and changed everything.

I picked it up again and put it outside my door. The smell of cigarette smoke and perfume drifted down the hall.

Suddenly I had one of those times when I thought about Dad. If he was alive, Mona wouldn't be here. We wouldn't be here. We never would have moved.

Mona's high heels clacked on the floor. I ducked back, leaving the suitcase out there. She might need stuff from it. I didn't know. The heels went into the bathroom. I heard the water running in the sink and then after a while I heard the toilet flush.

The metal gate over my window was locked like always, but the window was wide open. Only there wasn't any air to let in. I've got to get out of here, I thought. I checked the hall. Mona was still in the bathroom. If I really moved, I'd be gone before she came out.

Mom was standing by the sink.

"I'll see you later," I said.

"Sam!" Mom stopped me. "Ask July if he's got a fan or an old air conditioner in his bag of tricks. Tell him it's kind of an emergency."

"But then Mona will stay. Why don't you just tell her . . ."

"Her name's still on the lease," Mom said.

"Then let's pack and go back home."

"Someone else is living there now," Mom said.

"But, Mom, there's no room."

"We'll work it out somehow."

"I hate this."

"I do too, but Mona would never kick us . . ." She had to stop. Mona was out of the bathroom. "So, honey, remember to ask the super."

July wasn't in his office and the door to his apartment was shut. I stood for a moment in the basement and then I sat down in the swivel chair behind the desk. The lamp over my head made an island of light. Beyond that the walls turned corners and pipes disappeared into the shadows. I pushed off from the desk and the chair swiveled twice around. I tried again, pushing harder, going for three. I wondered what the world record was for swivel chairs. It was cool down here, about one hundred degrees cooler than upstairs, and it smelled of pine cleaner.

There was a newspaper in the mail basket. I swiveled around again. Then I heard the elevator. I put the paper back and got up just before the doors opened and July stepped out.

July's real name was July Sixteenth Simms. He had a sister back in Kentucky named September Fourth and a brother out in California named March Thirtieth. That's how his mother remembered birthdays. Every time I saw him, November Tenth flashed through my mind. That's what I would have been named if July's mother had gotten a chance to name me.

"The front door's on the fritz again," he said. "The toilet's plugged in 5D and the plumber's helper isn't helping. Always something. I need the snake."

"Mom said to ask you if you have an old air conditioner. Or a fan." I left out the emergency part. "I mean, it's no big deal if you don't."

"I've got everything," July said. "At prices that would put discount stores out of business. My last fan went yesterday, but I know I've got at least one air conditioner. It's a window model — work good in your place — that I picked up on Atlanta Boulevard last Thursday. Probably only needs a good cleaning. It's with the big ticket items in the back room." He pointed in that direction.

"I know," I said. "Thanks, July." July was cool. He was old, sixty or something, and I liked talking to him.

"But don't try lifting it." He punched the elevator button. "I'll get it with the dolly later."

There was some light from July's office behind me and a little more coming through the high casement windows, but I pulled light cords as I went.

Small rooms opened off one side of the corridor. In the utility room was a toilet and a sink as big as a tub. Then came the chair room and the lumber room, and then what I called the general junk room.

I took a look. July had brought in some new stuff since yesterday — a baby carriage, a wicker elephant table, and a birdcage. I figured that he had to be the world's champion mungo picker. He was always picking things up that other people had thrown out. He'd furnished his whole apartment that way. He said that anything anyone could ever want was out on the street somewhere. Especially Thursdays. That's when people threw out the best stuff. I'd started looking, but I hadn't found anything good yet.

The back room was the biggest, as wide as the whole building. I felt for the light switch on the wall.

The minute I turned it on, even before I had a chance to look around, I heard this rustling. Like rats. I'd never heard them in here before, but there were rats where I used to live as big as squirrels. I'd seen them, as many as four, crossing the street in a line.

Rats freaked me out. I wasn't going to fight them over any old air conditioner for Mona. I was about to switch out the light when the rustling came again. And then I heard a "Sssh," clear as anything.

The sound scared me stiff.

"Who's there?" I said. Nobody answered. I took a step back. "Okay," I said louder, "I'm going to call the super."

"Wait." A voice floated out of the corner like a ghost's. "Don't. Please."

I backed off another step. "This is a private basement."

Something whimpered. "Sssh," the voice said. "It's okay."

"I'm going to go get him now," I said.

"Wait." A black baseball cap and then a girl's face and shoulders appeared above the edge of an old bureau.

"Don't tell," the girl said. "I'm not stealing anything. It's only me and my dog."

3
. . . .

The girl reached up and pulled the visor of her cap down almost to her nose. I felt a cold, still place in my stomach. It was just the way Beans looked. The way she used to wear her hat, the one Dad got her at the baseball game. For a moment I couldn't speak. I couldn't even think. It was as if Beans had come back, as if she'd only been wandering somewhere in her cap for the past two years.

Then I heard a muffled bark. A little head bristling with rust-brown hair poked out of the top of the girl's jacket.

"Shut up, Harley," the girl said. The dog whined and licked her chin. Then he leaned his head toward me. His ears pitched forward almost like he recognized me.

"What are you doing down here?" I asked.

"I had to find a cool place. My dog's sick."

The dog kept staring at me. He had a fuzzy face and

a light brown nose and little black lips. And he was wagging his tail. I could tell because the front of the girl's jacket was moving.

"What's wrong with him?"

"Where's the super?" the girl asked.

"He's gone upstairs. But he'll be back. Any minute."

"Are you going to tell on me, or what?" the girl said.

I didn't answer.

"Because if you are, I'm getting out of here."

"How did you get in in the first place?"

The girl hesitated. "Just pushed all the bells till somebody buzzed," she said.

She didn't look much bigger than Beans, but I'd heard of kids even smaller than her mugging people. I wondered if she had a knife.

The dog whimpered and struggled inside her jacket. "He wants to get down." The girl edged out from behind the bureau. "So I'm going to let him. Okay?"

She was wearing funky pink sneakers. I relaxed a little. I figured I had a big edge on her.

The dog limped over to me and sniffed my ankle.

"Stop it, Harley. You don't know him."

"He doesn't act so sick," I said.

"He's got this heat rash," the girl said. "But mostly it's his leg. And he's hungry and he needs water."

The dog's hair stuck up in uneven tufts and there were lots of bald spots like he'd been shaved by a drunk. Then I noticed that a big patch of fur on one of his front legs was all scraped off and the skin looked like raw hamburger.

He jumped up and put his good paw on my knee. The other paw dangled. I knelt down to pat him. I couldn't help it.

Suddenly he was in my arms, trying to lick my whole face. His breath smelled like peppermint.

"He likes men," the girl said.

The dog started in on my ear. His tongue tickled.

"How did he get this skin thing?" I asked.

"He had it when I found him," she said. "But his leg is getting worse."

"Maybe you ought to take him to a vet."

"I can take care of him," the girl said. "Except he needs something to eat."

She'd said that before. It sounded like she was asking me for food. I thought about the snacks and sides and the chicken wings upstairs, but maybe what she really wanted was to get inside an apartment so she could rob it. I mean, she could have trained the dog to act friendly.

"What's your name anyway?" I asked.

"Oh, forget it," the girl said. She snapped her fingers. "Come on, Harley. Come here!"

Harley hopped down and went over to her. But before she could grab him, he turned around and came back to me. He went back and forth like he couldn't make up his mind. Then he took a detour over to the bureau and lifted his leg.

"Your dog's doing it on the furniture," I said.

"Harley, don't you dare," the girl said.

"It's too late." I almost laughed.

The girl bent down and scooped up the dog without

taking her eyes off me. He licked her chin furiously. "It's just because he so hungry," she said. "He needs a hot dog or something."

I thought of the pigs-in-blankets. "Don't you have food at home?" I said.

"No."

"No food?"

"I'm sort of on my own now."

"You mean you've run away?"

The girl didn't answer for a moment. "What's wrong with that?" she said finally.

"Nothing, I guess." I didn't know what else to say. "Except you're out of food. Just kidding," I added.

"That's not funny," the girl said.

I watched her tuck the dog inside her jacket.

"I guess I could bring some stuff down," I said.

"I don't want the super to catch me here."

Mom would kill me if I took her to the apartment, I thought. And maybe it was all a big trick. I didn't really know who the girl was. It's easy to lie, if you need help. But her story didn't sound like junk. Besides, I was a lot bigger than she was.

"I've got these pigs-in-blankets upstairs," I said. "They're like hot dogs, only little."

The girl stared at something to the left of me. "Is there anyone there?" she asked. "I don't want anyone to know about me."

I hesitated. "My mom's left for work by now," I said. "So you want to bring the dog up? For a little while?"

There was a 75 percent chance it would be okay.

4
....

The living room smelled of cigarette smoke and perfume and there were two half-full glasses of lemonade on the coffee table. But Mom and Mona were gone.

The girl came in slowly, only as far as the sofa, and stood peering around from under the visor of her cap. Harley was still wrapped inside her jacket.

I opened the refrigerator door. "There's the piggy platter." Mom had covered it in Saran Wrap. "And a couple of Chinese chicken wings. Eggs. Soda."

I piled food on the counter. "And there's this whole half a strawberry shortcake, and Danish. What does he want?"

The girl knelt down and unzipped her jacket. Harley struggled out and shook himself all over. He looked at me sideways and lifted his head toward the counter. His nose was twitching like mad.

The girl opened her knapsack and lifted out an oval tin box. It was white and gold and there were two angels with fat faces and big eyes painted on the cover. She filled the bottom of the box with water from the sink and set it down on the floor for Harley. He began to drink in little slurps. He had this funny stand-up tail that was thick at the bottom and curved over his back like a handle.

What a great little dog, I thought.

"Do you want to wash his leg?" I asked.

"He's got to eat first." The girl stood up and inspected the stuff on the counter.

"Those are turkey croquettes," I said, "and that's a fried wonton, but maybe he doesn't eat Chinese . . ."

"Harley, look," said the girl. "Baby hot dogs." She stuffed one of the pigs-in-blankets into her mouth and swallowed, almost without chewing. She ate two more. Then she put the last two into the lid of the box.

Harley sniffed them. Then he screwed up his face and sneezed. It sounded exactly like a person.

"That means he likes them," the girl said. She pulled one of the turkey croquettes apart, ate half, and added the other half to his dinner.

"What about these wings?" I pushed the plate toward her. "They're really salty."

"No chicken. Chicken makes him sad." But she picked up a wing and started tearing at it with her teeth.

"I guess he's a hamburger man, huh? Like me," I said.

The girl put down the bones of one wing and picked up another. "Somebody played a trick on him," she said. "They went off and left him tied to a bench with no water. That's when I found him. There were only some chicken bones in one of those cardboard cartons. If he'd eaten them, they would have killed him." She cracked the chicken wing into two jagged pieces. "See? Chicken bones splinter. It's like eating broken glass." She picked up the fried wonton and ate it in angry bites.

Then she began on the strawberry shortcake. I kept waiting for her to stop, but she ate the whole thing, except for a few fingerloads of whipped cream that Harley finished off. I'd never seen anyone eat that much dessert before, except for the time Lou dared Tommy to eat two dozen Dunkin' Donuts. But that didn't count because Tommy threw them all up.

She must be hungrier than the dog, I thought.

"Had enough, Harley?" she asked finally. The dog cocked his head. He had a blob of cream on his nose.

"Now I've got to fix your leg," she said.

The girl and Harley were still in the bathroom. I'd showed her the stuff in the medicine cabinet and given her one of my old T-shirts and a pair of scissors. Then she said okay, thanks, and shut the door in my face. I'd had time to put the kitchen back to normal so Mom wouldn't suspect anything. I even washed her and Mona's lemonade glasses with soap, because of Mona's lipstick marks. But I couldn't figure out how to get rid of the chicken bones. Suddenly they seemed like little sticks of dynamite. I was going to dump them, but then I remembered that dogs were always turning over garbage pails, so finally I stuck them in the drawer with the potholders until later.

I went and stood outside the bathroom door again. The water was running in the sink and the girl was talking to Harley. Her voice went on and on, over and under the sound of the water.

"Okay, Harley. . . . Don't be scared. . . . It's almost over."

For a moment I wished I hadn't let her close the door. Maybe she was swiping everything in the medicine cabinet.

". . . . I'm hurrying. I'm going as fast as I can," the girl talked on. "Okay . . . wait. I'm getting towels."

The water shut off and I could hear Harley's little whimpers.

"Good dog," the girl said. "That feel better?" The whimpering stopped. I tiptoed away from the door. After a while I heard the door open and then this little wet hairless body hobbled into the living room with his front leg all neatly bandaged. The girl had even made a sling. I recognized the neck band of my T-shirt.

"I used some of your Bacitracin," I heard the girl say. "The label says it helps prevent infection." She was standing in the hall doorway carrying her jacket and her knapsack. Except for her clothes I wouldn't have recognized her. Her face was scrubbed pink and shiny, but mostly it was her hair. It was short, almost as short as mine, but it was white — not blond, white. And her eyebrows didn't match. They were dark.

"You've got white hair," I said.

She put her gear down and pulled the black cap from the pocket of her backpack. There were these funny red blotches on her arms, like she'd caught the skin thing from Harley. "They told me I was bald until I was four. I guess it got this way because it was stuck inside my head so long."

In the cap she looked like Beans again. For a moment I wondered what color Beans's hair was now.

The girl zipped up her jacket. Harley sat down in front of her and waited.

I was half relieved that she was going.

"You can stay a little longer, you know," I said. "You want a soda? Or some lemonade?"

"We've eaten enough of your stuff. Thanks." The girl settled Harley into the front of her jacket. His bandaged leg rested in the open vee of the zipper.

"Where are you going?"

She turned at the door. "I'm meeting this friend."

"You know, my mom brings a lot of stuff home from the diner every night," I said. "I mean, if Harley needs food."

The girl hesitated. "If you tell anyone about me, they'll find me and make me go back."

She sounded a lot like Tommy, I thought. Tommy ran away, too, to Lou's house or to the roof. But nobody ever went looking for Tommy.

"I'm not going to tell."

"Okay," the girl said after a moment. "There's a place I go early in the morning. Trios, on Florissant Street. Near that big storage building."

"I know where you mean. I play ball there."

"So maybe I'll see you," the girl said.

"Bye, Harley." I only remembered after I closed the door that I didn't know the girl's name.

The view down from my window was blocked by the gate and the fire escape. I hoped maybe she'd cross over to the other side of the street. But she didn't. Then I had a Danish and some orange juice. Except for fruit, that was about all that was left in the refrigerator. If Mom asked about the rest of the food, I'd tell her, "You wanted me to eat, so I ate."

After that I watched the baseball game. The Red Sox were playing the Yankees. I hate the Yankees, but you had to like Don Mattingly. He looks like nothing, but he's awesome. Beans liked him, too. I remembered that she used to know all his stats, even better than me.

By the sixth inning the game had turned into a laugher. The Yankees were winning, 10–1. But I watched it all the way to the end anyway. There was nothing else to do.

Then I remembered the bathroom. I hadn't checked to see if the girl had swiped something.

The floor was still wet, but the towels were folded on the rack, really neatly, like a store. There were two flowered bags I'd never seen before on the back of the toilet. I peered into them. They were full of lipsticks and bottles — all of Mona's face stuff.

The girl hadn't taken anything. Even the tube of Bacitracin was still there in the medicine cabinet.

5
■ ■ ■ ■ ■ ■ ■

When I woke up the next morning, I was already sweating. Through my closed door I could hear snoring. For a moment I couldn't figure it out. Then I remembered Mona.

I checked Dad's watch. Only 6:15. He used to snore sometimes, but it never woke me up. I had to go back to sleep. What was I going to do with another whole day?

Then I remembered the girl. And Harley.

I pulled on my jeans. She might be there at Trios already, and if she was, she might not stick around.

Luckily I'd slept in my socks.

I tiptoed into the living room. Some lacy ladies' stuff hung over the back of a chair. Mona was this big lump under the sheet and Mom was this little line by the edge. I stepped over the end of the bed and Mona's suitcase and some shoes. Then I remembered the Danish.

I took two and a couple of apples. That was all I could

carry. Then I held my breath while I eased the bolt on the front door.

The elevator was slow, so I headed for the stairs. Suddenly I felt really sharp and excited, taking the steps two at a time, so silently, while everyone else was asleep.

Outside there was no one on the street and there were so few cars on Atlanta Boulevard that I could count them. The sidewalk was cooler than my room. My shadow stretched into the shadows of the leaves on the pavement.

When I reached Trios, the lights were on and I saw someone moving around inside.

It was the kind of place with booths on one side and stools at a long counter on the other. Two old men bent over coffee cups at the counter and a man in a white apron was setting pies and cakes under plastic lids. He watched me walk down to the last booth. A string of dingy gold bells and red letters spelling MERRY XMAS looped across the top of the mirror above the booths.

The girl wasn't there.

"Can I help you, buddy?" the counterman asked.

The air conditioner wheezed in the background.

"Yeah. I'm looking for someone. She has a dog."

"Dogs aren't allowed in here," the man said, "and there's a three-dollar minimum at the tables."

In the kitchen I heard laughter and the clash of plates and I could smell bacon cooking. Suddenly I was starving.

Then the girl came out of the back. She was wearing the same baseball cap, and her jacket was zipped right up to her neck, but I could see the bulge of Harley.

"I figured you weren't coming," she said. She stared at the apples in my hand.

"I've got a couple of Danish in my pocket," I said.

"Good. We'll eat outside." She scooped a whole handful of mints from the bowl by the cash register. I took some too, plus some toothpicks. When I looked back, I saw the man behind the counter frowning.

"He's not so bad," the girl said when we were on the sidewalk. "But the other one yells, 'cause I never buy anything. I only use the bathroom. It's got real soap."

Harley whimpered inside the jacket. "Oh, I forgot," she said and unzipped it enough for him to poke his head out. He looked really excited when he saw me.

"I didn't know if you liked apples," I said.

The girl nodded. "You want to go look at the river?"

We followed Twenty-first until we reached Shore Line. After that there were no more buildings, just a strip of green park along the water and the flatness of old wooden piers. We walked out onto one and the girl put Harley down. He hobbled across the boards as fast as he could, stopped, and hobbled back. I patted him and the girl fed him a mint. "That's all, Harley," she said. "They're bad for your teeth." He gave her a few quick licks and was off again.

I straddled one of the heavy beams that ran along the three sides of the pier. The girl opened the top of her knapsack and took out a plastic bag. "Don't look," she said. "This is private."

I tried not to, but I couldn't help it. It was only wet

laundry, a T-shirt and two pairs of pink underpants. She spread them on the beam to dry and then sat between them and me with her legs dangling over the edge.

Across the river the windows blazed with sun. There was a breeze and the sound of water lapping at the piles. But it was better to listen to it than to look down at all the junk floating in it.

The girl ate a pink mint. "You want a Danish?" I asked. I reached around. Gross! I was sitting on them. At least the plastic wrap had held. "Sorry. They're about ninety percent squished."

"You just scrape it off with your teeth," the girl said.

Harley hobbled back to us. He sat down in front of her and sneezed.

"You can have the outside," the girl told him, "but not the filling."

One Danish was nothing. Even though it was prune, I could have eaten five more. And drunk a quart of OJ. The girl was eating her Danish bit by bit. A crumb for Harley, a crumb for her. I tried to fill up on mints. The pink ones tasted just like the white ones. Why did they bother coloring them? I wondered.

I started on an apple. Harley watched me eat it. He kept sneezing, so I gave him a piece. That's when I discovered that he liked the inside but not the peels. He spat them out. It was funny.

"Do you come here a lot?" I asked.

"Sometimes. In the morning. It's quiet and nobody bothers me."

I stared across at the next pier. The piles slanted every

which way. It looked rickety and rotten, like it was about to collapse. I prayed our pier wasn't as bad.

"By the way," I said, "my name's Sam. What's yours?"

There was a long pause. "I'm not using it," she said.

How could she do that? Your name was your name. Whether you liked it or not, you were stuck with it.

"But what do your parents call you?"

She hesitated. "Different things. Baby, Missy, Jane. But I'm looking for a new one. I found Harley's on a motorcycle."

"Well, what should I use?"

"Don't you know any good names?" she asked.

It was a totally weird conversation, but I tried to remember the names of the girls in my old class and then I thought of Jill Anne. We'd never called my sister that. It was always Jilly Bean or Bean Bag or just plain Beans. But anyway, that name was taken.

"Wait a minute," I said. "When's your birthday?"

"December first," she said. "At least that's what they wrote down."

"Well, I know this man . . ." I told her about July's mother. "You could be December First, if you want," I said.

She looked down at the dirty water. "That sounds a little abnormal," she said.

"I'm named after my father," I said. "His name was Sam, too."

"My father was really nice," the girl said. "He had a beard."

"So how come you ran away?"

"I didn't run away from *them*!" She sounded almost angry. "They were the ones that had to leave."

"What do you mean, leave?"

The girl fed Harley another piece of apple. Then she picked him up and sniffed the top of his head. "You still smell good from your bath," she told him.

"They just left you?" I said.

"They had to. They didn't have enough money for a baby, so they had to leave me with people they thought would take care of me. It didn't work, but it's not their fault."

"But don't you care?" I asked.

"They're not gone for good."

"My dad's really gone," I said. "He died when I was eleven. He was killed by a car."

"They're sort of on vacation," the girl went on. "Right now they're in Mexico, maybe. Riding donkeys."

"It was a hit and run," I said.

The girl looked up. "You mean it was an accident?"

"Yeah, but it killed him anyway. And my sister. He was taking her out for meatball pizza."

The girl picked a piece of apple out of Harley's whiskers.

"My dad had to call nine-one-one the night she was born," I went on. "Or she might have been born in the elevator. He told me that story about a million times."

"What was your sister's name?" the girl asked.

"Jill Anne. But I called her Beans."

"December isn't a real name," said the girl.

"So you don't like it?"

"I didn't say that." She finished the core of her apple.

December sort of went with her hair, I thought. White, like snow.

"It's okay. I'll use it for now." The girl ate the crumbs off her jacket and collected her laundry. "Not totally dry," she said. "Tough." She stuffed it into her backpack and pulled out a crumpled shopping bag. "Okay, Harley." She picked him up. "I've got to go."

"Where to?" I asked.

"Get my coffee. Do my reading." Suddenly she turned on me. "I'm not ignorant, you know. A lot of kids like you, they think we are. Just because you have ritzy apartments."

"I never said . . ." Why was she so mad all of a sudden?

"The last school I got to go to, they put me in the sixth grade. I'm going to be a doctor. Maybe a veterinarian. If I was a vet, I could fix Harley's leg and his heat rash." She stroked his back. "Annie says that we have the same number of hairs on our body as dogs do. They just don't show because they're a lot shorter. I'll bet you didn't know that. And I'll bet you don't know what ostentatious means."

She was right. I didn't. "Who's Annie?" I asked.

"My friend."

I had to jog across the splintery old boards to keep up with her.

"And I've got to buy her more lipsticks and check the bulletin board and look for a leash and collar so Harley

30 ·

won't be so ostentatious . . ." She shot me a glance. "And I'm already late."

"Late for what?"

"Nothing." Then she stopped walking. "Do you know any jokes?" she asked.

"What kind of jokes?"

"Dumb, funny ones."

"Yeah. Sure."

"If you know some jokes, you can come with me."

We walked back along Twenty-first Street to Atlanta and then headed downtown. "Here." December handed me the shopping bag. "Hold this."

She bent over a trash can and began rummaging through the garbage. She came up with a couple of big plastic bottles and some empty beer cans. "That's five cents each," she said, dumping them into the shopping bag. "Thirty cents right there."

By the time we'd gone eight blocks, the shopping bag was full. "Maybe I'll do more this afternoon," she said.

Then she stopped at a place called Cooper's Café and pressed her nose against the plate glass.

"Good," she said. "He's still here." She turned to me. "Wait for me down the block. He doesn't know you."

I watched her from the phone booth on the corner. A man came out of the café. He was dressed in a hooded sweatshirt and pants so short I could see bright yellow socks. He handed her a paper bag. December opened the top, looked in, and nodded. Then the man shuffled off.

"Who was that?" I asked when December reached me.

"Big Bucks."

"So what's in the bag? Drugs?"

She frowned. "No. He used to be a banker."

I followed her across the street to a kind of island with a playground. She seemed so decided, as though she had everything planned out in her mind.

Through the links of a metal fence I saw slides and seesaws and things to climb on set in sand like a huge sandbox. A sign on the locked gate read "Reserved for Children and their Guardians."

The island widened out. December kept going, past another section with picnic tables along one side and a little wooden house in the middle with a flower box under the window.

Then we were in a small park next to the brick wall of an apartment building. Rows of giant trees with glossy green leaves grew out of the cobblestones. Under their branches it was darker and cooler and in the center there was even a statue of some guy on a horse.

It must have been a nice park once, but now the place was littered with newspapers and broken glass and there were people sleeping on almost every bench. One woman's legs stuck out from under the edge of a blanket. I saw the cracked soles of her bare feet. The man next to her was curled up on a mattress of cardboard boxes. He had a sweater pulled over his head.

It was scary. All of the people lay like they were dead. But I didn't know. They might rise up any minute, trailing stuff behind them, and come after me. I wished December hadn't cut through here.

Then I saw a woman at the far end of the park with her hands raised, as if someone had a gun in her back. She paced slowly across the cobblestones, a few steps in one direction, stop, turn, a few steps in another.

The woman turned another invisible corner and advanced toward us. Pigeons fluttered out of her way. I waited for her to turn again, but she didn't. Instead she kept coming.

Her face was gray, but her mouth was lipsticked as red as Mona's, And red lipstick slashes ran across her cheeks and her forehead. I geared up to run.

"December! Watch it. She's a crazy." But December didn't seem to care.

The woman came to a full stop. She stood there for a moment, only a few feet away, totally still. Then she put her palms together over her head and drew them down in front of her face. She bowed to December.

"Hail, Moon Queen," she said. "Thou that art highly favored."

December nodded. "Hi, Annie. I'm back."

6
....

I was sweating from the heat, but the woman was wearing an open parka over a sweatshirt. One skirt hung out from under another, there were a couple of scarves around her neck, and a white wool hat with a dirty pom-pom on her head. Her hair was wiry and stuck out almost sideways.

"Are you feeling better?" December asked.

The Annie woman stared past her. She raised her hands and brought her palms together again. This time she bowed to me.

"Hail, Samson, Lord of the Sun, come at last."

That really scared me. It wasn't my name but it was close. How did she know? Her pale blue eyes seemed to bore right through my head. I felt like she expected an answer, but I didn't know what to say.

"Hi," I mumbled finally. That seemed to work. At least the woman turned and started pacing her square again.

"How did she know my name?" I whispered.

December shrugged.

"But how?"

December shook her head. "Annie just knows things."

She went over to the bench under the tree and sat down. I went with her. I sure didn't want to be left out there in the middle of the park with a crazy. December lifted Harley onto the bench.

"What's she marching around like that for?" I asked.

"She's not marching. She's praying. And she's almost through. So move over. That's her place."

I stood up, fast.

A shopping cart was parked alongside the bench. It was packed full. A broom with its bristles sticking up was jammed down inside and a bright blue coat was draped over the top. The coat was really fancy with a fur collar and gold buttons.

"Don't touch anything," December said.

"I wasn't about to." Harley limped across the bench and leaned against me like he didn't see anything strange. Like everything was okay. I put my hand on his back and felt his skin stirring. "What did she mean, come at last?" I asked December.

She didn't have time to answer. The Annie woman was right there, looming over us. She smelled weird, not of sweat or dirt, more like raw potatoes.

She reached out a hand to pat Harley. There were deep black cracks across her palm.

"Big Bucks was there this morning," December said.

"Good," Annie said. "Now we can have breakfast." She straightened up. "Get the broom, Samson, and make the table ready." She unfolded the blue coat and flapped it out. December opened one of the brown paper bags.

"Am I supposed to sweep?" I whispered to her.

"Yeah. I get the water." She held up a green plastic bowl. "From the fountain. If it's working."

"But where? Where do I sweep?" I breathed.

"In front of her bench and under the tree."

I made a pile of cigarette butts and broken glass and bits of paper and swept the pile all the way to the edge of the park. A woman was asleep in an office chair by the curb. She was bent over with her head between her legs. The base of the chair was a big claw on wheels.

When I turned around, Annie had spread the blue coat on the ground with the sleeves stretched straight out, like someone lying on his stomach. December was nowhere in sight, so I waited.

The man on the bench nearest me was wearing a ski mask like bank robbers wear — to keep the light out, I guessed. I looked away in case he woke up and caught me staring at him. Then in the distance I saw December walking slowly between the rows of trees, carrying the bowl.

She set the bowl of water in the middle of the coat. I stuck the broom back in Annie's cart.

"Let Harley drink first," Annie said. Next to the bowl she put a pile of paper napkins. Then she went into her praying bit again, but this time she marched around the coat. "Praise to this moon, praise to this sun, and bless this water that we may drink." After she had circled the coat about ten times, she sank down all of a sudden with her back against the bench. The toes of her blue Nikes pointed straight up. "What did we get from Big Bucks?" she asked.

December sat down cross-legged and reached into the bag. I didn't know where I was supposed to sit. Finally I knelt on one of the blue sleeves.

"Two coffees," December announced, "two sandwiches — looks like cheese — raisins and peanuts, two cinnamon doughnuts, lots of packs of sugar and those little half-and-half cups, one plastic stirrer, mashed potatoes, and some meat gravy for Harley. Big Bucks said the coffee and doughnuts are from Cooper's. Everything else is from yesterday's soup kitchen. And I've got some mints." She laid them out in a white and pink line.

I'd eaten all mine. All I had left from Trios were toothpicks.

Annie poured five packs of sugar and four half and halfs into her coffee, stirred it up, took a sip, grunted and passed it to me. There was red lipstick on the rim. I thought of dirt and germs and disease. Annie smiled at me and reached for a doughnut. She looked as if someone had scrawled graffiti all over her face.

I turned the cup, closed my eyes, and took a quick gulp. It tasted sweet and creamy, like a melted shake. I passed it on to December.

"Give it back to Annie," she said. "I take mine black."

"Want to hear a good joke?" Annie asked. She didn't wait for an answer. "Two old folks were standing on a corner. One says 'Boy, were we poor when I was young.' 'So were we,' says the other. 'Why, we lived on Scraps for a month. Lordy, I loved that dog!' " She howled with laughter.

"Don't worry, Harley," December said. Harley lay by the water bowl with his head between his paws. His tail waved.

"I love jokes," Annie said.

"Tell her one, okay," December said.

"Me?"

"Yeah, you said you knew some."

"Tell! Tell!" Annie grinned at me. Her teeth were as gray as her face.

My mind went blank. I couldn't remember any of Tommy's jokes. All I could think of were dumb ones off cereal boxes. "What kind of a dog says 'meow'?" I said finally.

"I give up," Annie said instantly.

"A police dog working under cover."

"Under cover." Annie snorted and slapped her leg.

So I told another. "What's the best way to catch a rabbit?" Annie shook her head. "Hide behind a bush and make a noise like a carrot."

Annie laughed and laughed. December looked pleased.

"What do witches eat for dinner? Halloweenies!"

"Lor', lor'." Annie liked that one best of all. Even

December smiled. Then I ate a doughnut and half a sandwich and some peanuts.

"Here comes Satchel," said December.

I looked up. A tall black man with dreadlocks was headed toward us.

He stopped a few feet away and stood there, like he was waiting outside the door of a house. "May I come in, Annie?" His voice was soft and low and he had really brown eyes with white all around. "I have something for the little lady."

"A present?" December asked.

"It's something I found." The man fumbled in his jacket. "When I seen it hanging out of the can I says to myself, man, that little lady could use this here at-tacher." As he spoke, he began to pull something thin and green and long out of his pocket.

"A leash!" December said. "And a collar!"

"The end of the leash is broke," Satchel said sadly. "But I tied it real tight onto the other part."

"It's perfect," December said. "It's like a little harness, so it won't choke him. That's right, Harley, smell it. Look. See? It works. Thanks a lot, Satchel."

"You eaten?" Annie asked.

Satchel coughed. "I'm always partial."

"What's left, Samson?" Annie said.

"Oh. Let me see. A cheese sandwich, the doughnuts, some peanuts, a half-and-half cup, and the mashed potatoes."

"I'll take the potato. And the half and half. It goes down easy."

Annie gave him some napkins, too, and the tooth-picks, and then Satchel held up a hand. "I'll be seeing you," he said. I watched him walk away until he seemed to fade into the shadows.

Annie passed the coffee again. Pigeons cooed around us. Whenever they got too close, Annie threw a piece of leftover cheese sandwich over their heads. I ate some of the peanuts. If you didn't look around at all the people lying on the benches, it was like a picnic in the country with funny food.

Finally Annie rinsed her fingers in the bowl of water. She dried them on a napkin and wiped the corners of her mouth. "And they did all eat and were filled," she said.

I leaned back on my hands to stretch the kinks out of my legs.

"I'LL GET YOU, REBECCA!"

The voice was like a gunshot exploding next to my head. My heart stopped dead in the middle of my chest. "I saw you you thought I was sleeping but I saw you Rebecca crawling under my door stealing my things using my powder. . . ."

I scrambled back to my knees and shot a glance over my shoulder. The woman with the office chair was right behind me, screaming into my face.

"That's right YOU taking disgusting pictures of me for your dirty magazines. . . ." she shrieked.

I ducked away, but the yelling went on and on.

Then, "Rebecca is not here," Annie said, slow and clear.

But the voice never stopped or got lower. ". . . break-

ing my bed burning my furniture taking over my room
. . ."

Harley was up, barking. I could feel my face burning.

"Rebecca is *not* here," Annie repeated, louder. I saw
her blue Nikes move around the coat. "Go to Ninth
Avenue."

". . . swallowing my dreams I have you down on my
list . . ."

"GO!" said Annie. "And remember the white van."

The woman shut up.

I kept my head down. I could feel her still, right
behind me. Then I heard the wheels on the chair rumble
across the cobblestones. When the yelling began again,
it was far away. I risked a look. The woman was
pushing her chair along the fence by the playground.

"She wasn't talking to you," December said.

"Then who's Rebecca?" My face was still hot.

"The ghost who walks with her," Annie said. "Her
doppelganger."

"So now I've got to do my reading," December said,
"and return these bottles and look for a job."

I guessed the picnic was over.

Annie began to fold up the coat. Harley limped over
to me and put his good paw on my knee. I rubbed his
head. The Rebecca woman had disappeared. I saw a
lady pushing a stroller toward the playground with
another little kid hanging on to her free hand.

"I might be by the little house in the park later,"
December said to me. "Or I might not. Annie will
know."

That's when Annie went into another crazy act. I'd gotten sort of used to her, even the lipstick marks on her face, but suddenly her arms went up in the air and her palms came together and she was bowing to me again.

"Yes," she said. I felt my heart start up, she was looking at me so hard. "Go, Samson. It's time. Go and prepare a place for her."

7

■ ■ ■ ■ ■ ■ ■

I walked home angry at Annie and angry that my heart was still racing. Where did she get off telling me what to do? Besides, she was the farthest thing from a friend I could imagine. I thought she'd at least be a kid like December, not some old crazy living in a park.

I wondered if December was like Tommy. He hung out with some pretty weird people too, like the time he made friends with this drunk he met on the street. He even invited him home as a big joke on his father. Tommy was always doing stuff like that, but December didn't act like Annie was a joke.

And she sounded serious about a job, too. As if she planned to go straight into a big corporation. I almost laughed. She was too young even to do something little. And besides, they wouldn't take you at Burger King if you won't even give them your name.

There was a cart like Annie's parked outside my

building, but this one was filled with boxes of groceries. The delivery boy was getting buzzed in as I climbed the stoop. I caught the door before it swung shut and stood next to him waiting for the elevator. The guy held the box of groceries against the wall for a while and then he put it on the floor. When the doors finally opened, he pushed it in with his foot. We both stared at the numbers as the elevator rose.

"I quit after this load," he said.

"Why?" I asked.

"Two guys didn't show this morning. It's too hot. Things melt. Makes people mad, so they don't tip so good."

I eyed the box. It didn't look that heavy. The elevator stopped. The guy kicked the box out.

"What market is it?"

"Forget it, kid." He grinned back at me like he knew it all. "Even for this lousy job you gotta be sixteen."

He was still grinning when the doors closed. I wished I'd never asked.

"Oh, Sam, where have you been?" Mom said the minute she saw me. "Wait till you see what July's done."

The apartment was cold. I could feel the sweat drying on my face.

"Look what he's put in. An air conditioner. And he's only going to charge me forty-four dollars extra for the whole summer. Feel it! It even gets into your room." She twirled around with her arms spread.

"Where's Mona?" I asked.

"She went to check her apartment," Mom said. "Keep your fingers crossed."

The room seemed bigger, maybe because Mona wasn't there or because the sofa bed was folded up already or because the heat was gone.

"But where have *you* been?"

The buzzer rang.

Mom didn't answer it right away. She was holding her breath, I could tell. It buzzed again. She sighed.

"I'll bet it's Mona," I said.

"Be nice." Mom rolled her eyes at me. "Remember, it's still her apartment."

A moment later we heard thumping in the hall.

This time Mona was lugging two suitcases. One was so big it had those little wheels on the bottom.

"Good heavens, Mona," Mom said. "What's all this?"

"My clothes. What do you think?"

"But, Mona, that's enough stuff for a year."

Mona wasn't listening. "Thank heavens for July!" She flopped onto the sofa and toed off her high heels. "That air conditioner is bliss."

I backed as far away from her as I could get.

"But, Mona, where are we going to put it all?"

"Well," Mona said. "Pardon my garden. A body needs clothes, you know, unless you want me to wear my uniform day in day out."

"It's not that . . ." Mom began.

I stopped listening. I really wanted to stop being there at all. The room seemed to have shrunk back to even smaller than before. For the first time I noticed that there was only half a window left; the air conditioner blocked the rest.

Mom and Mona and I had lunch around the table by the window. Mona had to wear a dish towel over her shoulders because she said there was a draft on her neck. Her suitcases were stacked at one end of the sofa.

Lunch was roast beef sandwiches and Cajun bread pudding with bourbon sauce from the diner. The bread pudding stuck to the roof of my mouth and Mona's legs were everywhere. No matter how hard I tried, my knees kept bumping into hers and I'd jerk them back like I'd touched a hot wire. "Sam, don't rock the table," Mom kept saying.

Mona ate her sandwich and half of Mom's while she droned on and on about her landlord and the goons he'd hired to scare her off.

"Sam," Mom broke in finally. "Why so silent?"

"I'm not silent," I said.

"Bet he's thinking about girls," said Mona.

"He hasn't got a girl," Mom said.

"Wait," I said. "I want to ask you something. What does it mean when someone tells you to 'go and prepare a place for her'?"

"That's easy." Mona laughed. "She wants to marry you."

"Stop it," Mom said. "You're embarrassing him."

"Then it means go and find a good deal on an apartment with a decent landlord," Mona suggested.

"Everything doesn't have to do with you, Mona," Mom said.

"Well, la-dee-da."

"No, really, Mom."

"It sounds like the Bible," Mom said. "That time where Jesus is talking to his disciples and he says, 'In my father's house are many mansions; if it were not so, I would have told you. I go to prepare a place for you.' It's one of my favorite passages. I always see this big house."

"But, Mom, what if somebody said that to a regular person?"

"An apartment, like I told you . . ." Mona started to clear the table.

"I like to think that's where Beans and Dad are," said Mom. "In this wonderful house with a staircase like Fred Astaire danced down."

Mom was seeing death again. That was the trouble sometimes with asking her questions.

"Flo!" Mona shrieked. "Ugh! There are old dried-up chicken bones in the kitchen drawer."

"There can't be," Mom said.

"Well, what do you call these?" Mona waved a chicken wing skeleton under Mom's nose.

"Sam?" Mom said.

"This is so weird you won't believe it," I said. "I had this dream about chicken bones last night. They were huge and, and . . ."

"And what?" Mona said.

"And . . ." I'd run dry. "And they danced."

"Is that all?" asked Mom.

"What more do we need?" said Mona. "Where's your dream book? Check the numbers."

There was a number for "chicken" and a number for "bones," but no number for "chicken bones." They began to argue over which number to use.

"Mom, I'm taking some money," I said.

"All right, honey. Why don't you come by the diner later?"

"Maybe."

Mom kept bus tokens and loose change for me in a mayonnaise jar she hid in the freezer. I took a dollar's worth of icy cold quarters and a couple of tokens just in case.

When I left, she and Mona had written each number in the combinations on separate pieces of paper and were blind drawing them out of a cereal bowl.

In the downstairs hall I ran into July. "Mom loves the air conditioner," I said.

"All it needed was a new filter and more Freon," July said. "People are too impatient."

"I met another mungo picker," I said. "He found a leash for this dog I know."

"People think we're too cheap to buy new," July said, "but that's not it. We just hate to see good things thrown away because they got a little chip here or a crack there. Fix it up and there's no telling. Except for plastic. The world took a turn for the worse when they invented plastic."

"I'll keep looking," I said.

The street was broiling. That was the whole trouble with air conditioning. It set you up to expect cool. I was a sweat ball by the time I reached the park. The sandbox playground was deserted, but a bunch of kids squealed in and out of the sprinkler and a few adults lolled at the picnic tables.

December wasn't in front of the little house and she wasn't behind it in the shade either. I walked around it one more time to be sure.

Over the bulletin board was a miniature shingled roof and under it was the flower box filled with red geraniums. They looked like they were dying of thirst. I read the notices. "Wanted. Baby Sitter for *Adorable* Toddler. Call anytime. 555-9677." "Housepainter. Own drop cloths. Neat, Clean, Honest. Free estimates. References." All the little slips of paper with the painter's telephone number were still there. The suggestion box was stuffed with a pair of dirty underpants. That was it except for a mirror. I checked my hair.

The people at the picnic table got up and left without dumping their garbage. I looked at my watch. 3:40. There was a 90 percent chance I was waiting for nothing. I guessed I could go and ask Annie, but no way was I going to do that.

"Hey. Hey!" Someone must be yelling at one of the kids in the sprinkler. "Hey, you by the house. Samson! Over here." It was December, looking just the same, with her baseball cap pulled way down and everything. She stood outside the fence by the gate holding on to one end of a huge cardboard carton. "Westinghouse" was printed in big black letters across the side.

"Guard this," she said when I reached her. She darted over to the littered picnic table in the park and lifted the lid of the pizza box. Then I saw her pick up a leftover banana, peel it, and come running back. "I got lucky. This is the biggest kind of box," she said between bites. "The lid is thick and reinforced at the corners." She hung the banana peel through a link in the fence.

"Where's Harley?" I asked.

"With Annie. You can't take a dog on a job interview."

"A real interview?"

"Stupid lady." December sounded mad. "She asked a bunch of questions. Like phone number and references. All this dumb stuff that I don't have. And her kid wasn't so adorable anyway. She can keep her old job."

She must have answered the notice for a babysitter.

"There aren't any real jobs for kids," I said.

"There have to be. I've got to get some money."

"What about the bottles?"

"I already took them."

"How much?" I asked.

"A dollar fifty-five. I'll have to get out earlier tomorrow."

"I've got a dollar and a couple of bus tokens," I offered.

"I need more than that. Get the other end of the box."

We half carried, half dragged it. At the edge of the park a man was hunched on one of the benches, watching television. The set was hooked up to the wires in the base of a streetlamp. The picture was nothing but flickering light and lines, but I could hear the sound clearly. It was the Sox-Yankees game. They were in the fourth inning. The man coughed and spat onto the cobblestones.

December put the box down. "I've got to change hands," she said.

"What's this box for anyway?" I asked.

"For me. Annie said to find one. She said it was safer than sleeping out with her. She said they don't look in boxes."

"You're going to sleep out? In a box?"

"Yeah. People do it all the time. What did you think?"

I hadn't really thought. Maybe I hadn't wanted to think. But now it came crashing in on me. She was going to live in the park! Like Annie. Like all those other people on the benches. She had no place to go. No place to sleep.

I stared at her.

"What are you looking at?" December asked.

"Well, I mean . . ." I'd be scared out of my head, I thought. Of rats and weirdos and muggers. "Isn't it, you know, a little dangerous?"

"It's not so bad." She picked up her end of the box again. "Annie's always around."

"But what can she do? I mean, she's sort of crazy."

"What's so crazy about her?" December asked.

"Come off it," I said.

"She's not the least bit crazy," December said. "Not like the people I ran away from. They were really crazy."

"I'll bet they didn't smear lipstick on their faces."

"Let go of my box. I can carry it myself."

I hung on to my end.

"Let go!"

"I'm sorry," I said. "Okay?"

"You don't know *anything*," December said.

"I said I was sorry."

"You don't have to stick. Nobody asked you. I don't need a . . . a doppelganger, you know."

"Okay," I said again. "So where do you want the box?"

December stared at me a moment longer. Then she wiped her nose with the back of her hand. "Over by Annie."

"Okay."

But Annie's bench was deserted. Even her shopping cart was gone. Everyone was gone. The only person left was the man watching television.

"Where is she?" December looked around the park.

"Maybe she took Harley for a walk," I said.

"He wasn't walking so good." She pushed her baseball cap off her forehead. "Now what am I going to do?"

Then I saw Satchel, walking toward us really fast with Harley in his arms. He started to talk even before he reached us. "You can't stay here, little lady. Annie says to tell you that the white van is coming, so you got to stay away till they're through their business." Harley barked and scrabbled toward December. The sling and the bandage on his leg were gone. "Annie says to tell you right quick."

"Again?" December took Harley into her arms. He licked her mouth and her chin and then he turned his head toward me and sneezed. His green leash dangled all the way to the ground. "It was here only a couple of days ago."

Satchel shrugged. "It ain't me. It's Annie says."

"But somebody might steal my box," December said.

"Leave it lay," Satchel said. "You know well as I no one fusses with Annie's things." He began to edge away. "Pleased to meet you again," he said to me.

"What white van?" I asked.

"The city's." December examined Harley's leg.

"What happened to the bandage?" I asked.

"He pulled it off with his teeth when I wasn't looking. Do you think it's more swollen?"

It looked really puffy. "Maybe, a little," I said.

"No. It's really worse. I can tell."

In the distance I heard a yelling voice and the rumble of wheels on the cobblestones. "We'd better beat it," I said. "That Rebecca woman is coming."

"He won't put his leg down at all," December said. Harley stood looking deflated with his bad paw lifted.

"Maybe he needs an ice pack on it," I said. "Ten minutes on, ten minutes off, like for athletes. My dad told me that once."

A long drawn-out scream cut through the air. I spun

around. A police car, with its lights flashing, had pulled into the park. Behind it, by the curb, was a white van. Three people were struggling to get the Rebecca woman into it. Her chair lay on its side by the fence.

The woman never stopped screaming. It was horrible.

"Don't look." December had Harley in her arms. "Run! But don't look like you're running."

8
. . . .

The screams followed me to the end of the park. Then, as we turned the corner and the sun hit me and the building cut me off from sight, they stopped. For a moment it was like I was deaf. Except for the quick pad of my sneakers on the sidewalk and December's breathing, all the noise seemed to have disappeared from the world. Then, in the distance, I heard the wail of a police siren.

December slowed down. "Good," she said. "They've gone."

"What were they doing to her?" I asked.

"Carting her off to the hospital."

"But she was screaming. She didn't want to go."

December gave me one of her impatient looks. "They don't care. All they want is to make it nicer for the rich people. Rich people don't like to see poor people living on their streets."

Harley whined. "You want to get down?" she asked him.

He limped over to a fire hydrant and lifted his leg. When he was through he tried a few more halting steps before he sat down and refused to move. His ears sagged.

"Do you think that ice thing might work?" December asked.

"It worked for my dad, when he had his twisted ankle."

"Can you get some at your house?"

"We only have one lousy ice tray," I said.

"So now what am I going to do?"

"I know," I said. "The diner. Where Mom works."

"A diner that lets dogs in?"

"Oh, I forgot," I said. "No pets. No bare feet."

December hesitated for a moment. "How far is it?"

I had to think. "About twenty blocks."

"Well," December said. "At least we've got shoes."

We ended up taking the bus, but we didn't use my tokens. December said to save them for emergencies. The bus was so jammed that the driver didn't spot us when we slipped in through the back doors along with a man carrying a briefcase. Harley was a pro at buses. He hunkered down inside December's jacket and never even stuck his nose up to breathe. That's how we got him into the diner, too.

"Well, Sam, long time no see," Mona greeted us. "And who's this?"

Mom rescued me. She was carrying three full plates up her arm. "Oh, honey, you made it. I'm so glad, but I can't stop." She eyed December curiously. "And, Mona, your four top over there wants the check."

"This way," I told December. I led her between the counter and the booths to a small booth at the far end near the kitchen door. "This table is usually free," I said.

"What kind of a diner is this?" December said. "Tablecloths and candles and real napkins. And flowers. It's spastic."

"Wait till you see Manny," I said. "He's the owner. He has this gigantic hole in his ear. . . ."

"What about the ice?" December interrupted. She unzipped her jacket a couple of inches and peered down. "You said there was ice."

"I'm getting it, I'm getting it," I said. "You deal with Harley. Hang up your backpack. Act normal."

At the wait station along with the catsups and the mustards and the coffee and the salad dressings was a plastic tub full of ice. I used the metal scoop to fill two glasses and carried them to the table. December was sitting very still with her back to the rest of the diner. Her pack and her jacket hung from the coatrack attached to the booth, but Harley was gone.

"What did you do?" I whispered.

"He's on the floor." She looked straight ahead. "By my feet. I told him to be quiet. He's licking my ankle."

I glanced around. From the other end of the diner. Mona winked and waggled her fingers at me.

I wanted to give December a high five, but she was

trying to look so proper that I just pushed the glasses toward her. "Here's ice."

December popped a cube into her mouth and then spread her napkin on the seat beside her. She scooped ice out of the glass and rolled it up in the napkin. Then she disappeared under the table. "This is good, Harley," I heard her say.

I studied my menu even though I knew it by heart. There were some goofy sentences at the bottom, like "Eat your vegetables." "Stop scratching." "Don't let your chauffeur drink." "Clarence, call your mother."

That's when Mom showed up. "Sorry, honey, I've got two tables of picky people. But where's your friend?"

"She dropped her napkin," I said in a loud voice.

December popped up. The visor of her cap was knocked sideways.

"There you are." Mom sounded happy. "Don't worry about the napkin. I'll get you another."

December smiled at her. "Thank you very much," she said.

Mom beamed and dashed off. Harley whimpered. December ducked under the table again. "Stay, Harley. And shut up. You hear? Shut up!"

"Get back. Mom's coming."

"Here," Mom said. "Brand clean."

December smiled. "I've never seen such nice napkins."

"I'm so glad Sam brought you to the diner," Mom said. She was leaning over the table. Harley was right under her nose. "Do you live around here?"

"Mom, we're hungry," I said.

"Oh, of course you are." Mom took out her pad. "You want the usual?"

"Yeah," I said.

"I'll have the same," said December.

"And, Mom, some pigs-in-blankets, maybe?"

"I'll check with Salvi."

"And a milkshake," I said.

"Do you want chocolate, too?" Mom asked December.

"I'd rather have coffee," December said.

"Sure. All coffee? Coffee ice cream?"

I felt something brush my leg. Under the table Harley was moving around.

"Yes, please, thank you very much," December said.

"The same for me. Coffee," I said.

Harley barked. Mom cocked her head. Her pencil stopped in the middle of writing. I faked a coughing fit and at the same moment December faked sneezing. It was funny. But Mom was still looking around, behind her and at the floor. December put her elbows on the table and smiled really wide. "This place is so shiny and smells so good," she said. "It must be a scintillating place to work."

Mom's head stopped moving. She looked stunned.

"Why . . . well . . . that's so nice of you to say." She stared at December.

"Mom," I said, "we're really starving."

"Oh, yes, of course." She stuck her pencil behind her ear. "I'll be back in a minute with your shakes."

December waited until Mom was through the swinging doors. Then she leaned toward me. "Who's going to pay for all this?" she hissed.

"I do it all the time," I said.

"Then you must be really rich."

"Well . . . Salvi likes Mom. He's the cook. And sometimes he comps stuff when Manny isn't looking."

"What's that mean?"

"Complimentary. You know, free. Because Mom works here."

Harley gave another yip. December dove out of sight. "I told you to shut up. Now do it! Food's coming." She reappeared. "He doesn't like the napkin tied around his foot. How long has it been, anyway. Ten minutes you think?"

"Close."

December dropped out of sight. "Okay, Harley, you can take a break, but remember, be quiet. I think it's helping," she said when she was sitting straight again, "and besides it's really cold in here." She shivered.

For the first time I noticed how thin her arms were, sticking out from the sleeves of her pink T-shirt. Her elbows were so big and knobby, it was almost scary, like I could see how her arms were held together. The funny red blotches were peeling in places.

"I'm going to tell Annie about this place when I get back," December said. "She likes to hear about scintillating things. All the little details."

I hated it when she threw out those big words, like she knew more than me. "When did you first, ah, encounter

Annie?" I asked. "Make her acquaintance, I mean?"

"When I split, three weeks ago. She gave me two dollars for food before she even knew me."

"Here you go." Mom set two bulgy glasses on the table. "Two coffee milkshakes. And dressed pigs with mustard." She stood for a moment eyeing December. "You look familiar," she said. "Do you live in our building?"

"Mom. We're talking."

"And I'm interrupting." She smiled at December. "Mothers are all alike." She gave the end of the table a quick swipe with her apron and was gone.

"Does she live all the time in the park? Annie, I mean?" I said. "Like those other people?"

December didn't answer. I heard the noisy slurp of the straw at the bottom of her glass. Then she slipped two pigs under the table and ate a couple herself.

"Annie wouldn't eat these, not if you paid her. She likes pigs. She says they're really smart. She had one when she lived in the country, but it got killed when her house burned down."

Mom came back with plates of burgers and fries. She put the plates down quickly. "Salvi says 'hi,' " she said.

"Oh, good. Burgers." December picked up hers with both hands. She went right on talking between mouthfuls.

"Everything got burned up. All her clothes and her Bible and her grandmother's china and her kids' toys and her husband's important tools. So they came to the city to find work, but nobody wanted a Bible teacher and her husband didn't have his tools and then he got asthma and they ran out of money and they had to live in one hotel room with rats in the toilet. Then the kids were taken away by the foster people. So that was the end of them." December picked up the catsup bottle. "I only put it on my fries," she said. "If you put it on a burger you forget the burger taste."

Catsup was dripping through my fingers onto my plate. Suddenly, from way back, I had this memory of my first hamburger and how good it was and I decided that next time I was going to have mine plain, too.

"So then what happened?" I asked.

"They had to sleep under a bridge. Annie said she could hear the cars going by all night long right over her head. But she said it wasn't so bad there. The noise of the cars put her to sleep. But then her husband couldn't breathe and he died. And winter came and some guys beat her up one night. Annie said that's when she went a little crazy. She couldn't remember any jokes. So they tied her up in a hospital. That's how she knows about the white van."

"Is that what they did to the Rebecca woman?" The sound of her screams was still there, deep inside my ears.

December shrugged. "Maybe. But Annie's too smart. They'll never catch her again." Suddenly she began to shiver and her teeth chattered. She hugged herself. I could see goosebumps on her arms. "Stupid milkshake," she said. "I drank it too fast."

"You want something hot? I can get a cup of coffee."
She shook her head. "I'll be okay in a minute."

"Hey, big guy." It was Manny. He was wearing a white apron and a new earring, a little green plastic flashlight stuck through the enormous hole in his earlobe. "How're you doing with the numbers? Your mom's still waiting for a good dream." He laughed. "What's the matter? You don't like my burgers?" he asked December. "Eat up. You're as scrawny as a Perdue chicken."

"Does the flashlight work?" I asked.

"What do ya mean, does it work? I bought it special. Just put it in this morning." He bent down to give me a closer look.

"I like it better than the plastic banana," I said.

"Want to light my light?" Manny asked December. December shook her head. She slid her hands off the table into her lap.

Manny swung his heavy bearded face toward me. I pushed the switch as the flashlight earring lit up. I could see the bulb surrounded by a dazzle of light.

"Got to admit, better than candles." Manny laughed. "Won't blow out in a high wind." He switched off his flashlight and moved on to the next table.

"I can't eat any more," December said. She had half her burger left. "But I want to save it."

"Wrap it in your napkin."

"But the napkin's so nice."

"They have hundreds. Take the pigs, too," I said.

"For Harley. They just have to throw them out."

December made a little package and stuffed it into the pocket of her backpack.

"And can I take a menu for Annie? There are kind of jokes at the bottom."

"Sure," I said.

"And then can we go?" December said. "I'm worried about my box. I haven't had anything that good since they towed the car."

"What car? Can you *drive?*"

"No! You couldn't drive it. It was an old Cadillac wreck. But I slept in it for the first few days. With Annie. She let me."

"But I thought she slept on that bench."

"That's just for now. The car was before. She slept in the front and I slept in the back. On the floor under her blue coat, so when people looked in they couldn't see me. That's why the box is really important. Annie says they don't bother looking in boxes."

A box was better than a bench, I guessed, but still it was only cardboard and it was in the city. "It's still just a box," I said. "I mean, it isn't going to stop a guy with a knife who wants to get you."

December sighed. "I don't mean them," she said. "I mean the agency people. The people in the white van."

9
....

I stood guard by the table while December put on her jacket and made Harley disappear again, like magic, down her front. Mom waved from the window and December waved back.

"We were there for hours," I said, "and no one had a clue."

But December didn't smile or nod or anything. "Nobody ever has a clue," she said. Then she clammed up. For no reason. I wanted to ask more about the white van, but her eyes were hidden by the visor of her cap and her lips had disappeared into a thin line.

After a while she put Harley down and tried to make him walk on the leash. He lasted for about a block and then he lay down on the sidewalk and started to lick his leg. December had to pick him up again. Halfway back to the park she said, "Here, he's heavy," and handed him over.

He weighed more than I thought and he pressed like a hot blanket against my chest. I figured he must be broiling in what was left of his fur, but he acted really happy, like he loved me. He licked my chin and then worked his way up to my shoulder so he could lick my ear. I could have carried him a lot longer, but when we finally reached the park December took him back. "Everyone's here," December said. "The white van must be finished."

The television man was asleep on his bench and in the distance I could see Annie doing her praying bit again.

"I've got to set up my box now. Annie says it's going to get really cold tonight. And rain."

"You're kidding." The sky was totally blue.

"You'll see," December said.

"What is she, a predictor or something?"

"I liked the diner. Thanks." She started to walk away.

"We could go back tomorrow," I said, "see if Salvi can comp some dessert."

"Maybe." Harley wriggled in her arms and began to bark. "Oh, stop it, Harley. He hates it when people leave."

I could hear his barking all the way past the sand playground.

When I got home I turned on the TV. I was lucky. The Sox and Yankees were playing the second game of a twi-night doubleheader. In the eighth inning Don Mattingly went downtown for the Yankees with two on, tying his own record — ten homers in eight days. They replayed it over and over from every angle and then when the Yankees won 7–4, it turned out to be the game-winning RBI, too.

After that I watched part of a Japanese monster movie that I'd seen before and then I looked up "sintillating" in my paperback dictionary. It wasn't there. Ha, I knew it. She'd made it up. Probably "ostentatious" was fake, too. But I found it: "showy," the dictionary said, "attracting attention." Suddenly I wasn't so sure about "sintillating."

I turned the television on again and then I turned it off and wandered into the bathroom. All Mona's stuff was still there.

Mom had made my bed. The desk chair was pushed in and my bureau drawers were closed. That was one of Mom's things. She hated to see T-shirts and sweaters and underwear in a jumble. "It's like having dinner with someone who chews with her mouth open," she said.

I peered through the bars of my window gate. Same old fire escape, same old always-on streetlamp. Across the street a man in an undershirt sat in a lighted window looking out. He'd been there every day since we moved. Same man, same undershirt, same window. Like doing nothing was a job.

I wondered what December was doing in her box.

The box, I figured, was about 90 percent as big as my mattress. If I bent my knees I could fit in a place that size. And December was smaller. Maybe it wasn't that bad. And with a dog like Harley . . . a mugger might think twice. Still, I figured I'd be scared to go to sleep.

I lay down on top of my blanket. What had the people done to December to make her run away? What would I do, I wondered, if, let's say, Mom did something terrible to me? I mean, she got on me and sometimes I wanted to yell at her. And I'd had the urge to run sometimes. But I was still a kid. I wanted to enjoy life.

Maybe I just didn't have enough guts. I pictured December in the box with the backpack for a pillow and Harley curled up by her head.

Cardboard on top of cobblestones must be hard, a lot harder than my mattress. I rolled off my bed onto the floor and closed my eyes. There was no way to get comfortable. So I rolled over onto my red rug. Better. My hips didn't dig in so much. And with Harley lying against me . . .

"Sam. Sam! Wake up, honey." Mom was leaning over me. I scrubbed at my hair and squinted up at her. "You fell out of bed," she said.

I heaved myself back onto the mattress. "You smell like bacon, Mom."

She laughed. "Get undressed and go back to sleep." Then she brushed the hair back from my forehead and kissed me. "I'm glad you brought your friend to the diner," she said before she closed my door.

"I hate this weather." The voice was Mona's. I groaned and folded the pillow around my ears, but I could still hear her. "Broiling one minute, freezing the next. Why can't those weather people ever get it right? I'm going to make myself a cup of tea. Want one?"

Now I was wide awake and staring at the ceiling. Drawers opened and shut in the kitchen. Water drummed in the tub.

The smell of cigarette smoke and perfume seeped under the door.

Then in the distance, from somewhere downtown, I heard a siren. Before the sound had completely died away, without even knowing exactly why, I was out of bed and across the room.

As I lifted the window gate key off its nail, a flash of lightning lit the street like neon, followed by rolls of thunder. I'd never opened the gate before. The bars folded back like an accordion. I left the padlock on the chair next to the dictionary. The window rumbled going up, but the noise of the shower covered it. Then, just before I crawled over the sill, I went back and wedged the dictionary into my pocket and rolled up my red rug.

Through the metal slats I could see steps and more slats and steps all the way down to the pavement. For a moment I hesitated. If someone sees me, he'll think I'm stealing the rug and call the police, I thought. Then I remembered the man across the street. He was still there in the window. It was too late to duck, so I waved. He didn't move. He just sat staring. Maybe he was blind.

Outside the third-floor apartment I skirted a mop and a dead palm tree and then, on the next landing, the stairs ended. There was only a ladder, hooked to the landing above. I pushed up until the hook swung free, hoping it wouldn't make too much noise, and then the ladder went down with a scrape of metal on metal. In a flash I was on the sidewalk by the steps. Under the stoop, the barred windows of July's room were dark.

The streetlights and the doorway lamps made it easy to see, but still the night feel was there. I heard things, the wind in the leaves and my sneakers on the sidewalk and a scrabbling among the garbage pails. Either a cat or a rat. Better run, I thought. No, better not. If I ran, I might get really scared.

Traffic lights on Atlanta clicked from green to red to green as if there were a reason, but the street was almost deserted. Every now and then a car would come out of nowhere and pass on muffled tires like a ghost car.

A person huddled in a doorway surrounded by suitcases and shopping bags; another guy was asleep on the church steps. I paused. There was something familiar about him. Yellow socks. It was that man with the coffee. The one who used to be a banker. Big Bucks.

Then I saw two men halfway down the block. One was wearing a leather jacket and leaning against a building. The other was half hidden in the doorway. I slowed. They weren't talking. Just waiting.

Suddenly it was as if I could feel my blood beating in a hundred different places at once, even in the tips of my fingers. Don't look at them, I told myself. Keep walking. Act as if they're regular people, don't let them know you think they're muggers.

All I had was the quarters and the tokens and the rug. But they didn't know that and it could make them really angry. They might knife me for nothing. I held my breath. The two of them hardly gave me a look, but my back tingled all the way to the corner.

A gust of wind swirled sheets of newspaper around my legs. It was cold. I wished I'd brought a sweatshirt.

Lightning flashed above the buildings like fireworks and the thunder rolled again. Up ahead I saw the sign for Cooper's. It was still lit, swinging on its chains. I hitched the rug higher under my arm and tried a running jump as I passed underneath the sign. I felt my fingers touch wood.

Through the black links of the fence, the sand in the playground gleamed white. The little house looked abandoned. Then the trees of the park closed over my head and everything blended into the dark. It took a moment before I could separate the benches with their huddled figures from the tree trunks. "Hey, mister," someone whispered, "you got anything for me? A quarter? Any change?"

I kept going.

Annie lay on her bench at the end of the row. The broom in her cart stuck up like it was standing guard and her pom-pom hat was pulled all the way down to her nose. My sneakers made hardly any noise on the cobblestones, but somehow I had the feeling that she was awake and listening, like a lion, and knew it was me.

Then I spotted the box, against the building behind Annie's tree. It was tucked into an angle in the wall.

It was December's box for sure, right where I'd

figured it would be. A faint wavering light spilled out of the end closest to the wall. I crept nearer. Now that I was there, I didn't have a plan.

Then I heard Harley bark. The barking cut off and the light went out.

I knew December was keeping Harley quiet and wondering who was out here. So I knocked on the top of the box. "It's only me, Sam," I said.

10
. . . .

Harley came out first, this little limping dark shape. I knelt down and he tried to climb on me, sniffing and licking and sneezing all at once. It was like he hadn't seen me for a month. I rubbed his head and tried to kiss him back, but I missed. He was too excited.

I heard the sound of a match striking. There was a bright flare of light. It spilled out the end of the box and then dimmed to a glow. Harley stopped jumping and hobbled back inside. His front leg was wrapped and in a sling again. He looked over his shoulder to see if I was coming. I got down on my hands and knees and crawled into the box after him.

From the open end it was like looking into a smooth brown cave.

"I figured it was you," December said. She was sitting cross-legged all the way at the back with a notebook in her lap. "What are you doing here?"

I crouched at the entrance, half in and half out. "Nothing," I said. In front of her was a lighted candle stuck in a can and behind her her shadow was black and enormous. "I went down the fire escape."

"Lie down, Harley," December said. "I told you. You have to rest your leg."

I inched a little farther in. "You put the bandage back on," I said.

"I had to. He was licking it," December said. "And the worst thing you can do is let a dog lick a wound."

I sat on my heels and put the rug down beside me. My hair grazed the top of the box and I felt the cold air on my back. The candle flame wavered.

"I almost got mugged on my way here," I said.

"Yeah, well, it's dark."

December was wearing her jacket and under the brim of her black cap her face looked white and eerie. I shivered. I wished again I'd brought Dad's sweatshirt.

December closed the notebook. "So what's that thing?" she asked.

"Oh, this?" I said. "Just a rug."

"What for?"

"I thought, I don't know, maybe it might be good for Harley and you to lie on."

"Let me see."

I unrolled one edge. "It's red."

December moved the candle closer and inspected it.

"I don't know if it's going to work," she said, "but I'll try it. Move out, okay? And take Harley."

Outside in the dark, I sat on the cold cobblestones beside the box with Harley in my lap and listened to her bump around. Harley listened too. His ears moved one at a time, with every sound. Lightning glared for a second above the trees. "Okay," I heard her say finally.

The floor of the box was covered with rug. It looked as though it was made to order. Only a little curled up at the sides and at her end. In the light of the candle the red looked even redder. It seemed to fill the whole inside with color.

December was kneeling next to her backpack. "It looks almost like a real room," she said.

"And it's soft," I said.

"So, you coming in?"

The box was bigger than it looked from outside. I could sit cross-legged without my head touching the top.

Harley sniffed around in the space between us and then concentrated on one spot. "No, you don't," December warned. "You do that outside." Harley sighed and turned in circles until he lost his balance and fell over.

The box smelled new, like a can of paint that had just been opened. And there was something about the long cardboard walls, so plain and flat, as if they were waiting to be written on.

"I'm going to unpack my things." December sounded almost happy. "See what they look like on the rug."

What things? I only knew about the angel box and her laundry.

She pulled the box out of her knapsack first. Then three, four, five paperback books, a couple with no covers. She stood them in the back corner as though they were on a bookshelf. I read two of the titles, *All*

Creatures Great and Small and *Your Cadillac: The Owner's Manual.*

Then she took out a blue and white bandanna and carefully unrolled it. It was filled with little things. She moved the candle closer to Harley and folded the bandanna into a square. Then she flattened it out next to the books and arranged all the stuff on it. There was a green plastic letter "S" like the kind that sticks to the refrigerator, a tiny brown dinosaur, a miniature trailer truck, a Mickey Mouse figure, and a small fluffy yellow duck with orange feet and no eyes.

Lined up on the bandanna in the candlelight, the collection looked like the lighted things you see in store windows at night. The Mickey Mouse was the best. He had on little red shorts with two yellow buttons in front and enormous shoes like yellow rubbers and big white gloves. He was smiling and waving. "Can I see the Mickey?" I asked.

December hesitated. Then she picked him up by his waist and held him out to me. "The duck's from this Easter basket I got once, from my good foster family," she said. "I got to live with them for a long time. That foster father gave me the box with the angels when I got taken away again. All the rest I found in different places, but I can remember exactly where. Annie calls them my smalls."

Foster family. So that's who she'd run away from, I thought.

"This is a great Mickey," I said.

December took him back. "I found him first," she

said, "under a swing, forgotten. He was all dirty, but I washed him off. The bigger kids in the family I was with then would have swiped him."

Another family? How many places had she been? I pictured a mother and a father and a lot of kids with dark hair, and her. I wondered if the kids were mean to her because she was the foster kid and they were all real.

She stood the Mickey on the bandanna again with the others. "I had to hide him, but they weren't the worst foster family I had. One mother smacked me around a lot and the last mother put me in this tub of boiling hot water."

She couldn't mean it, I thought. "But mothers aren't allowed to do that," I said.

"Who's going to stop them?" December said it like it was every day normal. "They're bigger than me and have all the advantage. See?" She pushed up one sleeve of her jacket and showed me the red patches on her arms. The burn marks went all the way to her elbow. They looked like they must have hurt. "That's when I ran away, for good."

Behind me thunder cracked and rolled. Harley raised his head and barked.

"I think you were smart to split," I said.

December lifted the flap of her backpack again. "Where's my notebook?"

"Is it black and white?" I said. "Right behind you."

She twisted around. A ballpoint pen was clipped to the cover. "You're in here," she said.

"Where?"

A corner of the notebook was chewed and a lot of pages in the front had been torn out.

"Right there." December pointed. Then she turned her head away. "Comped," she recited, "means complimentary, free because you are related to someone who works there."

I tilted the notebook toward the candle. "Comped" was the last word in a column. Above it I found doppelganger and then ostentatious and at the top of the page I found scintillating. There was a "c" I hadn't figured on. "Sparkling, gleaming," December had written after the dash. The writing was script and the letters were small and neat.

I turned back a page. There were more columns. It was amazing. Some of the words I couldn't even pronounce. I thought about the dictionary in my pocket and was glad I hadn't brought it out and waved it in her face. "How old are you anyway?" I asked. She looked small, but her face could have been anything.

"Twelve," December said. "And a half."

"But how do you know all these words?"

"From the books I find. And Annie's been teaching me." December closed the notebook and propped it by the bandanna.

"Did you tell her about the diner?"

"She didn't want to hear."

"But did you show her the menu?"

"She wouldn't read it." December scrubbed her nose with the back of her hand. "She said she didn't have time."

"That's okay. You can show her tomorrow."

"No, I can't. She dumped it."

"Why? There are jokes on it."

"I don't know." Her voice was low. "She used it as a pooper scooper and then she threw it away."

There was a huge clap of thunder and then a soft tapping on the top of the box. It was raining. Harley growled and tried to get up. December put a hand on his back. "You've got to stay off your leg like the vet said."

"The vet?" I said. Big drops of rain splashed on the cobblestones outside. I moved farther in. It was really cold. The candle looked like it was giving out heat, but it wasn't. "How did you get to a vet?"

"I asked this lady on the street." December stroked Harley's head. "She gave me her doctor's name and told me to say that Harley was a friend of her dog Football. So I called and they gave me his emergency number. His name is Dr. Stern, but he was really nice. He said to bring my dog in first thing in the morning, but I said I couldn't because I had the flu and so finally he told me to wrap the wound in a clean, loose bandage so he couldn't lick it at all — I used up my other T-shirt — and to give it some support, and I've done that, and to make him rest for six to eight days. Right, Harley?" One of Harley's ears lifted.

"Rest? How are you going to do that?"

"I don't know. I haven't figured it out yet."

"He might fit in your backpack."

"I tried that already. He's too heavy for all day. Besides, he won't stay. He thinks it's a game."

The rain pattered softly right above my head. "I wish I had a cup of hot coffee," I said.

"So do I." December sat quiet. "I hope it doesn't rain too hard," she said.

I looked up. I'd forgotten the box was made of cardboard. "Should we cover it?" I asked.

"With what?"

I glanced around. There was nothing except the rug.

"Maybe it will be all right," December said. "Cardboard's not one layer, you know. It's a lot of layers glued together."

The ceiling still looked okay. It felt cool but dry.

December sighed. "You want a half of a half a hamburger?"

The roll was soggy and the meat was cold, but it tasted okay. I didn't notice until too late that December wasn't eating. She was feeding her half to Harley. Suddenly I thought of the refrigerator back at the apartment. It was nice to always have food at home.

"Do you realize that the only lipsticks Annie likes cost four dollars and ninety-nine cents each," December said, "plus tax? And I've only got ninety-five cents left because I used two quarters on the phone calls."

"Why does she need them?" I said. "Why does she do that to her face?"

December shrugged. "She just has to. I think she likes to look angry."

"But why?"

"To scare people. To keep the creeps away. Annie never sleeps at night, you know. If you think she's asleep now, you're wrong. She says it's too dangerous."

So I was right. She was out there, guarding, with her face all war-painted like some kind of old-time Indian. I wouldn't mess with her, even without the lipstick.

"Why didn't it scare you?"

"It did," December said, "in the beginning, but then she called me Moon Queen, like I was important, and lent me the money." She paused. "And I got used to her. But I don't know now. Something's happening to her. I thought she was okay yesterday when you came, but she's gotten sad again. She's run out of lipsticks and she says she's too tired to buy them. So I've got to get more, three at least. She'll be all right if she's got lipsticks. I just know it."

"I've got a dollar and those tokens." I shifted onto one hip and fished them out of my pocket.

For a moment I thought she wasn't going to take them, but then she did. "You sure you don't need it?"

I shook my head.

She crossed her arms and hugged herself. Her teeth were chattering. "I'd better tell you something," she said. "I already got a lipstick from you."

"What are you talking about?"

"I took one," December said. "From your bathroom that time. I didn't mean to, but there were so many right there in the bag. And Annie's already used it."

I had to think. "Oh, that's only Mona's stuff," I said. "I wish you'd taken them all."

"I've written it in my book," December said.

"You don't have to. Really."

"And I'll write in your quarters and tokens, so I'll remember to pay you back. And I owe Annie. A lot. It's up to five dollars now."

Harley barked in his sleep and his back legs ran. December stroked his head until he stopped twitching. The candle had burned down almost to the top of the can. I checked Dad's old watch. 4:35.

"I've got to go," I said. "I left the ladder down."

"You want to borrow my raincoat?" December asked.

She handed me a black plastic garbage bag. "I'll put it on outside," I said.

"I'm glad you brought the rug," December said. "Thanks. It makes it warmer."

It was still dark outside and freezing and the rain hit me in big drops. But no way was I wearing a garbage bag home. I took a last look into the box. Harley was barking and the tiny Mickey was waving. December raised her hand. "Bye."

"See you tomorrow."

I started across the park with my shoulders hunched and my head down. That's why I almost ran into her.

"Samson."

I nearly stopped breathing.

Her Nikes planted on the rain-slick cobblestones looked black and her skirts were wet and dragging. I clutched the garbage bag against my chest.

"The Moon Queen is more than forty camels' burden," Annie said. "You have to get her off my neck."

I swallowed. "You mean December?"

The lipstick marks were dark slashes on her face, but she wasn't using her fierce crazy praying voice.

"I feel doomed," she said. "I cannot help the Moon Queen anymore."

I tried not to look at her. It was raining harder now. Heavy cold drops hit the top of my head. I glanced back, but the light in the box was gone. "But what am I supposed to do?" I shivered and hugged the garbage bag closer.

"Take her off the street," Annie said. She sounded quiet and sad, like anybody.

"What are you talking about?" I took a step back. "How?" My legs were shaking.

"Find a way. My money is run down and I have to go."

"But you can't. You're her friend," I said. Suddenly I was desperate. "And I don't have anyplace to take her."

"Anyplace is better. Even the white van," Annie said. "She won't last on the street."

She started to walk away.

"There's no room in my apartment."

She didn't even bother to turn her head.

"I'm just a kid," I shouted at her back.

She kept walking.

I stood for a moment, alone and shivering. It seemed a long way between the park and home. Suddenly I felt there were people out to get me, all around me on the benches, ahead of me in the shadowed doorways and creeping up on me from behind. I started to run.

11
. . . .

By the time I climbed back through my window, I was totally soaked. I stripped and pulled on dry underwear and Dad's old sweatshirt and kicked my wet clothes under the bed. Then I rolled myself up in my blanket and lay with my face to the wall.

I was so tired I couldn't believe it. From the neck down I ached to go to sleep, but my brain was wide awake. It wouldn't stop thinking.

Annie was going to split. She wanted to dump December on me. That's what all that stuff about "go and prepare a place for her" meant. She wanted me to take over.

But how could it be me? Annie was even crazier than I thought. I didn't live in the park. I didn't know zilch about finding food or making money. I'd never even collected bottles. And I couldn't bring December here. The place was too small already. Besides, it wasn't even ours. It was Mona's. Mona could kick us out anytime.

I climbed out of bed trailing my blanket. Drops of rain bounced off the slats of the fire escape. The man across the street was gone — probably asleep. Mona was snoring in the living room. The sound made me feel worse; everyone was asleep but me.

I stared at the bare floor where the rug had been.

Maybe there was someone, a city office or something that was in charge of finding places for people. Mom might know. I could ask her and call.

Dumb! That was so dumb! They'd have questions and if I gave them answers, they'd send the white van and December would end up back with that terrible foster mother. It would be like turning her in. She'd hate me for life.

I lay down again. I had to sleep before I could think, but I had to stop thinking first.

Maybe Annie didn't mean it. Maybe she was just sad, like December said, because of no money and no lipsticks. Maybe lipsticks were really that important to her.

But Annie hadn't said one word about lipsticks to me. I could still hear her voice. "Get her off my neck." She had sounded calm and sure.

My brain swung around again. What if Mom left me? I thought suddenly. What if she disappeared like Dad and Beans and there was no one in the next room, no next room, no walls? If I was like December, alone outside, what would I do?

I tried to imagine and then I gave up. There were too many things to be afraid of. Suddenly I was so glad that

I was inside with real walls and a real ceiling and a bed and a refrigerator and a television and a mom, even though she bugged me sometimes.

All December knew were bad places and bad people, except for her parents way back and the angel box father and Annie. And now Annie wanted to leave, too. It wasn't fair.

I started to cry. I cried for a while, but it didn't help. Lying in bed wide awake didn't help either, so I got up again.

The man was back in the window across the street, sitting there, staring at nothing. Why didn't he do something? Why didn't somebody do something? Why did it have to be me?

The streetlight went out. Above the buildings the sky was a pale gray, almost white. It was already morning. I'd been up all night.

I went back to bed and rolled myself into a ball again. After that I conked out for a while, but I kept waking up. I heard the toilet flush and Mom and Mona padding around. I heard my door open. I lay still with my eyes shut and made myself think of nothing. Later the door opened and closed again. Finally I gave up.

I found dry socks and my older pair of jeans and pulled them on. My sneakers were cold and clammy, so I left them under the bed to dry some more.

Sheets of rain swept across the fire escape.

December's cardboard box. That was another thing. How long would a box like that last? And she didn't even have that stupid garbage rain bag. I pressed my forehead against the metal gate until it hurt.

My door opened. "Oh, you're up," Mom said. "You had me worried. It's almost noon. I kept coming in to see if you were breathing like I did when you were a baby."

"Where's Mona?"

"Don't worry. Not here. She's at a tenants' strike meeting in her new building and she won't be back until tonight. Come on. I've got a surprise for you."

The living room was all decorated, like someone was having a party. There were three bright red pillows I'd never seen before on the sofa and flowers everywhere — purple and white ones, and a bunch of red roses in a big glass jar — and two presents wrapped in purple paper on the kitchen table.

"Who are the presents for?" I asked.

"You and me," Mom said. "From Mona. She won the lottery again and she spent it all on us. A hundred and twenty-five dollars! I don't know how she keeps winning. She got the number from this dream she had about a mobile home that went over a cliff."

"But why? What's it all for?"

"She said, sort of a thank you, for letting her stay. See? I told you," Mom said.

One of the presents was big and lumpy. The other was small and flat. "This is really nice of her," I said, "but I'd rather have her go."

"Me too," Mom said. "Mine's the little one."

I ripped off the paper from the lumpy present. It was a first baseman's glove, a really good one, a Don

Mattingly. His signature ran right across the pocket.

I couldn't believe it. It was even a lefty's. Mattingly and I were the same that way. "Hey!" I said. "This is so great."

"She asked me what you'd really like," Mom said.

I slipped my right hand in. The glove felt tight and stiff and smelled of leather. I pounded the pocket with my fist.

Mom laughed and held up a scarf. It had this swirly pattern in three different shades of purple. "I'm going to wear it to the diner. Who cares if it doesn't go with my orange vest."

She wrapped the scarf around her shoulders. "Now, what do you want to eat? I got prune Danish, of course, and an onion bagel — I gave the other one to July — and a big container of chili. And yesterday's special dessert, Death by Chocolate Cake."

"Maybe just OJ," I said.

"Not even some cold cereal?"

I shook my head.

"You feeling okay?" Mom asked.

I nodded.

A little later she asked again. "You sure?" She leaned across the table and felt my forehead. "No fever."

I pulled my head away. "I told you. I'm fine." I put the glove back on. It wasn't that bright orange color, like a kid's glove. It was dark brown and hand-stitched and the leather creaked.

"I liked your friend," Mom said. "She was so well spoken."

"Yeah, well . . ." I wanted to tell her, I wanted to ask. But it was like I had this tight heavy ball in my stomach. "Mom, what if I wanted a dog? Could we ever have one? Here, I mean."

"Oh, hon." She spread her hands and shrugged. "Where would we put it?"

"I mean a little dog."

"But even a little dog costs money. They have to eat and go to the vet's and get shots. Right now it's more than I can handle."

"But what if it was an emergency?"

"Now wait a minute. Are you talking about a dog or are you talking about Mona living here?"

"I don't know." I pounded the pocket of my glove. "I was just wondering if we could ever get a bigger place."

Mom sighed. "Maybe someday. If we win the lottery."

I stared at the air conditioner. The windowpane above it was streaked with rain. I wished I was sixteen, I wished Dad was here, I wished I'd never met December, I wished . . . I didn't know what I wished.

"But, Sam, honey, it's not your worry. Mona won't be here forever. I hope," she added under her breath. She gazed down at her hands. For a moment they lay on the table as if her fingers were too heavy to move. One of her knuckles was red and there were wrinkles around her wrists I'd never noticed before.

Then she leaned back and said, "You look tired. Sort of like a boiled owl."

"Good. I like owls," I said.

"I think I ought to call Manny and tell him I can't come in."

"No. I just need to sleep some more." I wouldn't go back to that park ever, I thought. Then Annie would give up on me and she'd have to stay.

I let Mom set me up on the sofa. "This way you'll be near the telephone and the TV," she said. She stacked the new cushions on the kitchen table and brought me my pillow and her pillow from the top of the closet and a blanket and a pile of comic books.

Finally she left.

I lay on the sofa fooling with my new glove. I'd give it the water treatment and then as soon as it was broken in, I'd try it out on the warehouse wall. The only problem with the water treatment was that after you'd really soaked it you couldn't use the glove for at least three days. It was even better if you left it tied around the ball for a week. I pounded the pocket and listened to the sound of the rain drumming on the air conditioner.

December's rain bag was under my bed. I groaned. I prayed that the box was okay or that she was sitting at the counter at Trios with Harley inside her jacket having coffee. Dry and warm. Maybe she had another place to go. I didn't know everything about her life.

The telephone rang. Mom calling already to see how I was. "I was sound asleep," I said into the receiver.

"You still are. This is your bad dream calling."

"Tommy! Hey, where've you been?"

"Where have *I* been?" Tommy drawled. "Right. Sure. You were supposed to call us, don't you remember?

When you got your phone. I had to call the operator."

"So, I was just gonna call you guys. Really."

"Great!" Tommy said. "So call." He hung up.

It took a moment and then his number came back to me. The phone rang about ten times, but no one answered. I didn't know what to do. Then my phone rang again. "The number you have reached has been changed to 555-5565." It was Tommy, trying to sound like an operator. "Please make a note of it." Then he hung up again.

I redialed.

He was howling with laughter and I could hear Lou yelling in the background.

"Cool it," Tommy said to him. "Not yet." He came back on the line. "So how's the new apartment?"

"Pretty small."

"You mean so small that the rats have to . . ."

"It's not so bad," I said. "But, hey, where are you?"

"Two blocks away. In a phone booth."

"You want to come up?" I asked.

"I don't know. You could come here. Cram in with us. But Lou hasn't had a shower in weeks, so maybe your place would be better. You got any beer? Lou wants to know."

"I do not!" Lou was yelling again.

"Sure," I said. "A case of Bud Light."

"Be there in ten seconds," Tommy said. "Starting now."

I just had time to get rid of the pillows and the blanket before the buzzer rang.

We ate the chocolate cake and all the chili, cold, right out of the container. Then Tommy found an open pack of Mona's cigarettes on top of the toilet. "She'll never miss 'em. Smokers never count."

He smoked two by himself. I'd smoked one once, up on the roof at the development, but I didn't like it. It was a big nothing. I didn't even get sick.

Lou took a drag and then passed. "If Mom smells it on me, she'll break my head. She thinks everything's drugs and pot." He looked at Tommy. "So are you going to tell him?"

"I don't know yet."

"Tell me what?" They'd been hinting at something all afternoon.

"Where's your glove?" Tommy asked. "I want to try it again." He was a lefty, too. "You got a ball?"

We played catch until Lou went out for a pop fly and knocked over the jar of roses. The new red cushions got all wet, but luckily the jar didn't break.

"It's stopped raining," I said. "Let's move it outside. There's this place I know."

It was gray and misty and the air smelled good. All the garbage in the gutter had been washed down to the drain at the end of the block. The rain was like a fine prickle on my face, not enough to wet the glove before I was ready. But I didn't want to take any chances. "Give it," I said to Tommy. I put it under my sweatshirt.

We walked right past Trios. I thought of sneaking a peek through the window, just to see if December was there, but instead I ducked my head and speeded up.

When we got to the warehouse, Lou drew an imaginary line on the wall. "That's the center field fence," he said. "Anything gets over that, it's a homer."

Then we took turns making these leaping death-defying catches. For the first time since we moved I felt like it was summer.

Lou was the best even though he was a righty and couldn't use the glove. He was taller than me and a lot taller than Tommy and he could hang in the air like a basketball player.

"Hot hands! We got hot hands here!" he kept yelling.

"The line's too high," Tommy said, so Lou lowered it, but he was still the best. "Gimme the glove," Tommy said to me. "Feed me some grounders."

He couldn't miss.

"Man, am I tough with this glove," he said. "Is it cool! I'd sure like to have it at the park."

It made me feel good. Usually nothing got to Tommy.

"So now are we gonna tell him?" Lou asked. "I mean it's getting late."

"Okay, okay. Don't have a hernia," Tommy said. "Look, it's like this. Lou's brother is putting together a scratch game tomorrow afternoon at that field the college uses. You want to come? He says we can play."

"Sure, great," I said.

"There's definitely going to be beer." Lou grinned.

"And you got to let me wear the glove," Tommy said.

"How come?"

"You wouldn't have known about the game except for me."

"The guy's hardly even used it," Lou said.

"Tell you what," I said. "You can have it for an inning. Lou too. But give it back now. Before you forget."

Tommy pulled it off reluctantly.

We started toward the subway station. I pounded the glove as I walked.

Then, two blocks from the station, we turned the corner and there was Annie. Right in front of us.

I went cold. It was like she knew, like she'd been waiting for me. She was wearing her same hat and that bright blue coat with all the gold buttons done up.

I panicked. I thought about turning around and running or cutting across the street into the traffic, but then I'd have to explain to the guys. They were already looking back at me. All I could do was keep walking. I kept my eyes on the pavement and prayed Annie wouldn't say anything.

But she started to shuffle along beside us. Out of the corner of my eye I could see her big blue Nikes. "Who's your friend, Lou?" Tommy asked.

"Cut it out," Lou said. "Can't you see?"

I'd seen. It looked like she'd tried to scrub off the lipstick lines, but all she'd done was smear them. Now her whole face was painted red.

"She's all duded up for you," Tommy said. "A real princess." He was dancing along sideways.

"Cool it," Lou said.

The subway was a block away. If I could only get them there.

"Sorry, lady," Tommy said to Annie. "My friend's not interested. Better get a real job." He turned to me. "That's what my dad tells 'em."

"Samson?" Annie said.

It was the worst thing. My face burned.

Tommy stopped. "She's talking to you."

"No. She isn't." I was cringing inside.

"She is too!"

"Come on," Lou said. "Back off."

"Samson," Annie said again.

"Who-ee," Tommy said. "She even knows your name."

"That's not my name. She's making it up. I've never seen her before in my life."

"Don't mess with her," Lou said. He tugged Tommy

away. "You never know what they'll do."

"She doesn't scare me," Tommy said. "She's nothing. My dad says they're all drunks and druggies." He shook Lou off, but at least he kept going.

"Stop bugging me," I whispered to Annie.

"Samson, I see desolation and destruction and brimstone and the sword."

"Shut up with that wacko stuff," I said. The guys were almost at the subway.

"A bad time is coming," Annie said. She stopped walking. "And I'm tired, but I can't lie down. I've got to keep moving on. The Moon Queen will come to harm."

I speeded up. I couldn't see her Nikes anymore.

But her voice followed me. "Samson, please. I've lost all my jokes."

At the subway steps Tommy said, "Remember, bring the glove." Then he laughed. "But don't bring 'beet-face.'"

I wanted to laugh with him and I wanted to punch him out. I felt caught. "They're not all druggies," I said.

"So, we'll see you tomorrow," Lou said.

I wondered if December knew Annie was after me. I wondered if she knew Annie was planning to leave. "Wait, you guys. I just remembered," I said. "There's this thing . . . I mean I can't go."

"What! To the game?" Tommy stared at me.

I stared back. I couldn't believe I'd said it. "I forgot," I said. "I've got something I've got to do."

"You kidding?" Tommy said.

"No, I'm not kidding." I wanted to feel good about it, but I felt miserable.

"Hold it," Lou said. "Are you okay, man? Are you in trouble?"

"Not me," I said. "But somebody."

"Is it your mom?" Lou asked.

I shook my head.

"Then can't you put it off?" Tommy asked. "What's more important than a game?"

"This thing," I said.

"Boy." Tommy spun away. "What a dumb move."

"I'm sorry," I said. I meant it. I figured I'd be even sorrier tomorrow.

"Don't sweat it," Lou said.

"He's probably got a date with 'beetface.' " Tommy stomped down the subway steps.

Lou shrugged and grinned and gave me a high five. I watched until they disappeared.

When I turned around Annie was gone. I was glad. I'd turned down the game to do something about December, but I didn't even know what that something was.

13
■ ■ ■ ■ ■ ■ ■

After that I just walked for a while. I didn't really know where I was going, but I ended up sitting on the steps of a library. The library was closed, but I didn't care. All I felt like doing was nothing.

I sat with the glove in my lap thinking about the baseball diamond near the college. It would be a good game. Usually only the rich kids got to use that field. There was still time, I thought. I could change my mind.

I fingered the laces on the glove. It was stupid to have turned down the game. I wondered what Don Mattingly would do if he were me. He'd probably go, I thought. He was always taking extra batting practice.

Maybe I could write to him about December. He might dedicate a game to her or something. Tell all the reporters he was going to hit a homer for her and then point to the bleachers like Babe Ruth did and knock one out. And there would be pictures in all the papers of her and Mattingly, and December would be famous and people would send her money and offer to adopt her for good.

Except a kid had to be in the hospital or dying for something like that to happen.

That got me thinking about Annie again, and then I stopped. I didn't want to think anymore. So I sat and stared at the cars going by and the people and the library steps. It was nice sitting there, not trying to figure out anything or fix anything, just letting time go by.

"Excuse me?"

"Huh?" I'd forgotten where I was.

"Excuse me, but are these your steps?" a lady asked.

"Uh, no." I stood up, feeling sort of embarrassed. "But the library's closed."

"Now that's too bad," the lady said. "I think that libraries and churches should always be open, don't you?"

"Yeah, I guess," I figured she was a teacher, and then I saw her legs. They were all swollen and purple and she was wearing an old pair of bedroom slippers. Two bulging shopping bags rested by her feet.

"When I was your age they were," the lady said, "but I suppose it's too expensive now." She started up the steps. "You wouldn't happen to have a match, would you?" Without thinking I felt my pocket and then I shook my head. "Or some extra change?"

"No." I backed onto the sidewalk. I'd given all my quarters and tokens to December. "I'm sorry."

"That's all right. Thank you anyway." The lady turned away.

You couldn't tell anymore, I thought, about anyone.

It was raining again. Not hard, but enough to make rings in the puddles by the curb. I looked back. The lady was spreading layers of newspaper on the top step under the shelter of the archway over the library door.

"When I was your age," she'd said. She was once a kid, just like me. It was hard to believe, but she had a nice face, normal, not lipsticked up or anything. Like Mom's.

Suddenly I didn't want to hang out anymore. I wanted to go straight to the park, but I didn't have December's rain bag. So I headed home to get it. And maybe I could raid the mayonnaise jar for a few more quarters.

A few more quarters wasn't much, but the thought of giving them to December made me feel better. I tucked my glove under my jacket. At least I was heading somewhere. Like Mattingly when he was in a slump, going down to the batting cage and hitting off the tee. He just plugged away until he got his eye back and could make something happen.

And suddenly I got my eye back, too. I mean, at least I figured out the first thing . . . Annie had to stay. No matter what. Even if she was wacko and sad, she had to. And I had to think of a way to make her.

Lipsticks. She was out of lipsticks. December said that if Annie had new lipsticks she'd be okay again. It sounded far out, but maybe it would work.

So, all right. Buy lipsticks.

I multiplied it out. With tax, three lipsticks came to

about fifteen dollars. Counting my quarters, December had a dollar ninety-five now. There was more in the mayonnaise jar in the freezer, but I couldn't take it all. Figure another dollar there. So that left twelve plus I had to find somewhere. And soon.

July was standing on the sidewalk in front of the stoop next to a big white dishwasher or something and a delivery cart full of grocery boxes. I saw him scratch his head. Then he saw me.

"Yo, Sam. Just the man I was looking for."

"Me?"

"I need a strong arm to help me with this dryer. Someone dumped it out with the garbage." He gestured toward Atlanta. "Want to bet it only needs a fan belt? I got it this far with the dolly, but I need a hand up the steps."

"Sure," I said. "Did you see my new glove?"

July admired it. "Isn't that something," he said. "Are you going to soak it?"

I nodded.

"I'll give you some neat's-foot oil, better than linseed. You rub it in good."

July opened the door of the dryer and felt around inside. "Clean as a whistle," he announced. "Put your glove in here. Now, grab the front, I'll handle the back in case it slips, and be sure to take the weight in your legs."

"I remember," I said, "from when we moved the sofa."

The delivery boy from yesterday was coming out. July got him to hold the door. I stared at him, but he didn't remember me.

We wrestled the dryer up the stoop and into the hall. Then I tipped it and July slid the dolly underneath again. "Keep a hand on it," he said, "to steady her."

In the basement we rolled it out of the elevator and toward the back room where I'd found December and Harley. July walked backward pulling the rope on the dolly and I pulled the light cords. As we rattled past the general junk room I peered in. The weird wicker elephant table was still there and so was the birdcage and now there was a big box stuck head first in the baby carriage.

You know how sometimes you see something you've seen before and suddenly it looks entirely different? That's what happened when I saw that baby carriage.

July and the dryer rattled on to the store room. I ran to catch up. "Hey," I said. "That baby carriage you found. What's wrong with it?"

"Nothing," July grunted. He tipped the dryer and kicked the dolly away. "A front wheel is all."

"That sounds like a lot."

"It's only one out of four," July said.

"Can you still push it on three?" I asked.

" 'Course," July said, "but why would you want to?"

"Because I need it. I mean, if you don't want it?"

July stared at me. "If it's not too presumptuous," he said finally, "could I ask why?"

"For this friend . . ." I paused. At least I could tell him about Harley. "Who has this dog with a bad leg."

"How soon do you need it?" July asked.

"Pretty much now."

July whipped a screwdriver out of the slot in his pant leg. "Just let me take the back off this here machine, see if I guessed right."

I went for the carriage. The carton was heavy, but I got it out and put it on the floor. It was full of old copies of *The National Geographic*. The carriage was dark blue and padded on the inside and it had a carrying case hanging from the handle and a wire rack running underneath. But it was actually missing two wheels, because all the others were doubles, like a semi.

"I was wrong," July said when I returned with it. "The fan belt's fine. This machine is as good as Gussie's horse. Probably people just wanting to buy new." He sat back on his heels. "Now . . ." He inspected the carriage.

First he measured the wheels. Then he disappeared up front and when he came back he was carrying a wooden box. "My wheel collection," he said.

There were two sets that fit. I picked the white walls.

"Okay," July said. "Axle through this here hole in the leg tube. Put the wheels back on, one on each side, make sure they're even, then you're ready for the stop nuts." He shuffled through the box and then he got up and disappeared down the hall again. He came back with a paper bag. "My stop nut collection," he said. "You pop them on. That's all there is to it."

"What are the red things between the wheels?"

"Brakes. See, if you press the pedal down they flip on. If you press the lever they flip off."

He handed me an oil can. "Give it a good squirt. Don't be shy."

"They're working," I said. "They spin like crazy."

"This is a good carriage," July said. "It'll corner like a race car." He checked it out, tightening bolts with his wrench. "Uh, oh," he said. "There's a rip in the hood."

I wanted to get out of there, get the carriage to the park. The hood didn't matter. "I don't care about that," I said.

"But the dog might. Go get the duct tape. It's silver, on the desk in my office."

He showed me how to tape the tear on the inside so you could hardly notice. "An invisible mend," he said.

"This is great," I said. "Thanks a lot, July."

July rolled the carriage back and forth. "There we are. One Rolls-Royce fit for a — what kind of a dog did you say your friend had?"

I didn't know. "A combination dog."

"— fit for a mutt," July said.

I checked Dad's watch. It was getting really late.

"Can I owe you, for the carriage I mean?" I asked.

"What time do you have?" July asked.

"Ten after eight."

"Give me a hand with one more job and we'll be square."

I hesitated. "Will it take long?"

"No," July said. "It'll take short. There was a washing

machine next to that dryer. They shouldn't have put it out until tomorrow. Thursdays are the days for bulk pickup, but if I don't go back and get it now, one perfectly good washer might end up in the city dump."

It took a lot longer than a few minutes. By the time we hauled the machine back to the building in the rain, the streetlights were on and I was feeling really antsy.

July tipped the washer off the dolly next to the dryer.

"Two for the price of none," he said, "and no little thanks to you."

I opened the door of the dryer and took out my glove. "I think I'll take the carriage now, if that's okay." I had to drop off my glove and get December's rain bag.

July nodded. "I'll go up in the elevator with you. I've gotta ask 3A if I can have that plant on the fire escape."

"But it's dead," I said.

"You never know."

Then, when we were in the elevator with the baby carriage, July said, "Speaking of fire escapes, there's a city ordinance. You're not allowed to go up 'em or down 'em unless there's a fire or some such thing." The elevator stopped at three and the door opened. July stared right at me. "Sometimes I forget to tell people and they get into trouble that way." He patted the hood of the carriage and stepped out.

The elevator creaked upward. He knew about me, going down the fire escape, I thought. Maybe he'd been looking out his front window or the people in 3A had heard me and told him. I couldn't be sure, but I figured I'd better not use it again.

The elevator doors opened and there was Mom. Mona's scarf was tied under her chin and the minute she saw me she burst into tears.

"I thought something terrible had happened to you," she sobbed. "I kept calling and calling but nobody answered. I thought you were so sick you were unconscious. So I came home and your rug was gone and all the pillows were wet . . ."

"I'm sorry. I was helping July," I said.

"Why didn't you call me? Where have you been? And what are you doing with that baby carriage?" The doors started to close. Mom pressed the button to stop it. "Get out of there," she said.

I pushed the baby carriage into the hall. Mom leaned against the wall and put her hands over her face. I hated it when she looked so crumpled.

"I'm sorry," I said again. "I forgot. Tommy and Lou came down and we were hacking around."

"I've told you and told you . . ."

I waited while Mom found a Kleenex and blew her nose. "I wish . . ." She took a deep breath. "I wish I wasn't like this. I get so panicky about you I can't think straight."

"Your scarf's coming untied," I said.

Mom pulled it off. She gave me a watery smile.

"The guys wanted to play ball so we had to go out," I said. "And then I had to help July move stuff."

"I'm such a fool," Mom said.

"No, you're not, Mom. Not all the time."

"Well," Mom said, "one good thing. I'm not going

back to the diner tonight. We can have an evening together. Without Mona."

This was the worst thing. How was I going to get back to the park now? I stared at the baby carriage, trying to think.

"I could make us some spaghetti," Mom said, "and maybe there's a ballgame on TV."

There was no way out of it. I tried to look glad.

"But what are you doing with this carriage?" Mom asked again. "Is it July's?"

"I'm supposed to deliver it," I said, "as soon as possible."

"Not tonight, please, hon. It's raining and dark."

I wheeled it into the apartment.

"Oh," Mom said, "can't it stay in the hall?"

"No. It's a really good one. It might get stolen."

I put the carriage in my room and Mom made spaghetti and I set the table and then we watched the last game of the Sox-Yankees series. I sort of watched without seeing. I thought about Lou's brother's pickup game and I thought about December in the park and I thought about Annie. There were two rain delays. The Sox won 7–6 even though Don Mattingly got a double in the bottom of the ninth. The announcer said he'd gone four for four, but I couldn't remember his other hits.

As soon as the game was over, I said good night to Mom and went to my room. The carriage looked funny, parked in the corner. I wondered what December would say when she saw me with it. First I'd tell her it was for Harley like I'd told July. She'd be impressed. She probably wouldn't say anything to me, but she'd clear it with Harley. And then I'd tell her she could buy all the stuff Annie needed.

She'd look at me sideways from under her baseball cap and say, "With what?" And then I'd tell her my other reason for fixing up the baby carriage.

14

·······

The next morning I had to pick up the carriage and lift it over the pullout bed. There wasn't enough room to wheel it past. Mom's eyes opened. "Sam?"

"It's okay," I whispered. "I've got to deliver this, remember?" I put the carriage down and opened the door.

"But what about breakfast?" Mom elbowed herself up. "There was a special on fruit."

It was easier to do it than argue. I loaded up on peaches, maybe December would like them, and a grapefruit and three apples. One was for Harley.

There was no Danish.

"What's this stuff wrapped in tinfoil?" I whispered.

Mom peered over the lump of Mona. "I haven't the faintest. But take it. Must be from the diner. Are you coming home for lunch?"

"I'll call. Promise."

"Last night was fun," Mom whispered. She snuggled back down and blew me a kiss.

Outside it was cool and sunny and clear, like the city was starting over. It was a little after seven, so the streets were pretty empty. A few people were walking their dogs, but I was the only one with a baby carriage. After a couple of blocks I stopped and put December's rain bag and the food in the carrying case. I didn't want to look like I was taking a bunch of fruit for a walk.

I wheeled past Cooper's. Ahead of me I could see the big trees. Maybe December was already up having coffee.

But when I got there it was all different. There was no one in the park except for the man with the TV and one lady pulling clothes out of a busted shopping bag. Annie's cart with the broom sticking up was parked alongside her bench, but her bench was empty.

December's box was still in the same corner by the building, but it looked abandoned. The top sagged and the sides bulged and in places it was stained a darker brown. But where was she? I never thought that she wouldn't be there.

The lady with the busted bag turned toward me. "Taking your little sister for a walk?" she asked.

I nodded. "All my things got to dry," the lady said. She pulled something gray out of the bag and wrung it out. Water dripped onto the cobblestones.

Maybe I'd passed her. Maybe she was in Cooper's.

"You looking for somebody?" the lady asked.

"A friend," I said.

"Most of them's gone to the shelter," the lady said. "Not me. Got my shoes stolen last time I went there. But they'll be back. They get thrown out at six thirty."

I felt so relieved. I smiled at her.

"You got nice teeth," she said. "Mine all went bad."

I braked the carriage by December's box and looked at Dad's watch. 7:45. I hoped she'd be here soon. The television man sipped from a paper cup and stared at his TV set. But it wasn't working, not even the sound.

Then I heard a noise from inside the box, like a muffled cough or a bark. Harley! I ducked around to the open side, but there was nothing in there except for my red rug all rolled up at the far end. The bottom of the box was cold and soggy and the sides were all blotched and mottled like they were rotting. I started to back out and then I heard the sound again. "Harley?" I said.

The rug moved. I saw his nose work its way out.

"What is it?" December's voice said. The rug heaved and then unrolled and there she was with Harley's leash knotted around her arm.

"Oh, hi," I said. She rubbed her eyes and pulled at her cap.

"Has it stopped raining?" she asked.

"Yeah," I said. "Did you get wet?"

"I guess I fell asleep." Her voice sounded stuffed up like she had a cold. Harley whined and hobbled toward me.

"I tried to get back last night. Really." I scratched Harley's head. "But my mom . . ."

"I'm freezing," December said, "and the rug's wet."

She crawled out, dragging the rug after her. Harley squatted and peed on the cobblestones. December's eyes were red and her nose was runny and her chin looked blue.

She coughed and peered over at Annie's bench. Then she saw the carriage. "What's that?"

"It's for Harley," I said. "I found it yesterday."

December sneezed. She put a finger under her nose and sneezed again.

"That was part of what I was doing last night. I saw it and I knew. You can push him everywhere and we won't have to carry him. I had to fix the front wheel."

December nodded. "That's smart," she said.

"And it's got safety straps," I said. I'd just noticed.

"Really smart," December repeated. "Want to try it, Harley?" Harley yawned and licked his little black lips. December plopped him in. "They're like a seat belt. They clip to his harness," she said.

Harley sniffed at the straps and the sides and the folds of the hood. He sneezed and his ears perked up.

"You got a Kleenex or a paper towel?" December asked. "I used up all the napkins from Cooper's."

"No, but I brought your rain coat and some fruit and some stuff from the diner and . . ."

December turned away and blew her nose onto the cobblestones. Then she wiped her nose on the back of her hand. "My feet are cold," she said. "I wish I had socks."

"You can have mine, but they probably stink."

"I don't care."

I moved the carriage over by Annie's cart. Harley sat up straight with his bandaged leg across his chest like he was saying pledge allegiance to the flag. December spread the red rug over the back of the bench. I gave her my socks. She didn't even bother to smell them.

"I'll write them in my book," she said, "so I'll remember to give them back." The heels came up above her ankles.

"Where's Annie?"

"She's not here," December said. "But she'll be back."

"When?"

"Probably soon."

"You sure?"

"Course I'm sure. It's Thursday, right? There's this place that dumps their day-old bagels and on Thursday there's always a lot of whole wheat raisin. Annie's crazy for whole wheat raisin." December jounced the carriage. "You want to go for a roll, Harley?"

I wanted to tell her about my other plan, but I had to see if the carriage worked for Harley first. December took him for a trial spin to the end of the row of trees and back. Harley peered over the side, watching the cobblestones go by.

"Now he's sure to get well," she said. "He doesn't even notice he can't walk." Harley sat bolt upright like he'd just been elected king of the dogs.

"There's something even better," I said.

"Like what?" said December.

"Like a way for us to earn money."

That's when I told her.

At first she didn't get it. "It's stealing," she said. But then she pushed her baseball cap up and her eyes got wide. "No. It's more like helping," she said. "The delivery man just gets done quicker and goes back for more. It might work. Why didn't I think of that? I'm strong."

"I didn't think of it either until I saw the carriage."

"I wonder if anyone's ever thought of it before?"

"Maybe we're the first people in the whole world," I said.

"I'll bet we are. And I don't need an address and I don't need a phone number and it doesn't matter how old I am." December rocked back and forth, her hands squeezed between her knees.

"I know."

We stared at each other.

Harley gave a little yelp from the carriage. "You want some fruit?" I asked him. I fed him a piece of apple with no skin.

"So let's do it," December said.

"It's only 8:20." I handed her a peach. "I don't think they start until around eleven."

December coughed and rubbed at her nose. "I *hate* waiting," she said.

While we waited, we turned December's box bottom side up, so it could dry. Then December folded the red rug and slid it into the carriage under Harley for extra padding. "It's dry enough," she said. "And Annie doesn't like other people's things touching her bench."

We took off at 10:15. December couldn't wait any longer.

"Besides, we'll need time to find a market, and scope it out." She left a peach for Annie in her cart.

Harley rode and December pushed and I walked alongside like we were a funny family.

"There's the Alpha Beta," December said, "but the Associateds are bigger. Or maybe we ought to stick to markets near Pleasant Avenue. That's where the rich people live." Then suddenly she stopped and turned the carriage around. "I know," she said. "Washington Market. They dust their fruit with this feathered thing."

Washington Market had a green awning and stands of fruits and vegetables on either side of the door. A truck was pulled up in front and two men in dark green jackets were off-loading boxes down a ramp into the basement. December wheeled the carriage by slowly.

"See," she said, "I told you."

I saw boxes filled with food lined end to end down an aisle. The floor was covered with sawdust.

"They're all ready to go." December pushed the carriage to the end of the block. "We can sit on the steps of that church across the street. Everyone will think we're extra religious."

We'd hardly sat down when a two-wheeled wooden cart, painted green, rolled out the market door. A man leaned his weight against the handle.

"Look at him," December said. "It must be really full."

Another cart with another man shoving came right behind. He turned the other way.

"Quick," December said. "Which one?"

"The first. It looked heavier."

The cart made a lot of noise. We could follow it without getting too close. The man pushed it around a corner and a few moments later the rumbling stopped. The cart was parked, tilted forward, in front of a town house. The man lifted the green cover, took out a box and went down the steps. December wheeled closer. Harley sat straight and still, except for his ears.

The door buzzed and the man disappeared.

"Okay. Now!" I said.

December pulled up alongside the cart. I raised the lid, grabbed the first box and dumped it in beside Harley. He gave a surprised bark. December had the carriage moving already. We ran until we reached the end of the block.

"Okay. Now where's the label? What's the address?" she asked.

"Crawford. One forty-seven South Eleventh Street. And there's a number two. What does that mean?"

December took a look. "It says *'number of boxes — two'!* Oh shoot," she said. "There must be another one."

I never raced so fast in my life. The second box was right on top and this time I remembered to close the cover of the cart. I didn't notice how heavy the box was until I was forced to slow down. December helped me stash it on the rack underneath the carriage.

"It weighs a ton," she said. "It's nothing but melons and bottles." She coughed and blew out her nose again.

One forty-seven was a fancy doorman building.

"We can't let him see the carriage," December said.

"I guess I'll have to take them one at a time," I said.

"Why not me?"

I knew there was a reason. I thought for a moment. "Because I've never seen a delivery girl."

"You just want to do it because it's your idea."

"It's not that," I said. "He might be suspicious. You'd be too . . . ostentatious."

December smiled. Not a big smile, but a smile. "Take the old box. I don't care. I'll wait around the corner."

"I'll be back for the melons."

The doorman watched me lug the box toward him.

"What do you think you're doing?" he said. "The service entrance is around back."

"Sorry," I said. "I'm new. Where's the back?"

"The way you came," the doorman said.

December looked surprised when she saw me. "What happened? Why didn't you leave the box?"

"Couldn't," I panted. "Wrong door."

The back entrance turned out to be better anyway. No one was guarding the door. I carried the box down the steps and through a gray corridor until I found the elevator. I left it there and went back for the other one. Harley barked at me and wagged his tail.

The elevator man wore gray pants and a gray shirt. The address of the building was written on his pocket in black script.

"Delivery for Crawford," I said. The man nodded and watched me drag the boxes in. Through the elevator gate I watched the floors and the numbers drop by. We stopped on the sixth floor. The elevator man latched the gate and got out too. I hadn't counted on that. It made me nervous. I wondered if he did it all the time or whether it was just because of me.

The doorbell rang inside the apartment. I waited for what seemed like ages. I rang again. Then I had a horrible thought. What if no one was home? Would I have to sit and wait with the boxes? Then I heard footsteps and someone fumbling with the lock.

The door opened. It was only a kid, really little, five maybe six. I looked behind him. There was no one else, nothing but this huge kitchen with a black-and-white tile floor and glass cabinets and two refrigerators.

"Oh, the food," the boy said.

I'd never thought of a kid. It wasn't in my plan. Kids don't have money. I'd lugged the stupid boxes for nothing.

Then I heard a woman's voice from somewhere in the apartment.

"Norton, darling. Who is it?"

"The food boy," Norton bellowed.

"Oh, dear. Tell him to wait. I have to find my bathrobe."

Maybe it would work after all, I thought. I carried the boxes in.

"Wait," said Norton. "Mummy said wait."

The elevator man and Norton waited with me.

Norton fooled with an elastic band and the elevator man leaned against the doorjamb. No one said a word. The kitchen was painted a shiny dark green and mirrors ran everywhere behind the counters and the sinks. There was a built-in TV and a wooden table with a sofa on one side and chairs on the other and the stove was huge and black and had red handles. A whole family could have lived there, I thought.

Finally I heard high heels coming. Then this blond lady in a raincoat hurried through the door carrying an open purse. "I couldn't find my bag," she said, "and now I've lost my wallet. No, here it is."

I stared at her white shoes. It was working. I was actually going to get money. I tried to act bored.

"Oh, dear," the woman said. "Do you have any change?"

"Change? No," I said. "This is my first delivery."

"Don't look at me, Mummy," said Norton. "You never pay me back."

The bell in the elevator rang.

"Oh, dear," the woman said again. She glanced at the boxes and then back at me. "Aren't you young to be doing this?" she asked.

"I have to work," I said. Then I lowered my voice to make it sound sadder. "It's just me and my mom."

The bell rang again. Behind me the elevator man shifted his feet.

"Oh, well," the woman said. "Here. But this will count for the next few times, too."

"Thanks." I took the money, but I didn't look at it. I

stared right at her nose. "Thanks a lot."

I didn't look down, not even in the elevator, not until I reached the steps to the street.

Harley lay with his chin resting on the rim of the carriage. He struggled up when he saw me.

"What took you so long?" December demanded. "Did you deliver them? Did you get anything?"

I grinned at her. "This." I dangled the ten-dollar bill under her nose. "Get a load of this!"

15

December took the ten, stuffed it into the carrying case with the food, and snapped the flap shut.

"Our bank," she said.

"This is incredible. And we've just started," I said.

"I'll bet this was a one-timer," December said. "Like when Annie got a new twenty from this woman with little diamonds on her stockings."

"But delivery boys work until seven. I've seen them. So after we get the lipsticks to Annie, we can . . ."

"There's an Associated we passed a couple of blocks back," December interrupted, "and a Romano's on the corner of Fifteenth and Hillcroft. Let's try them next."

We never got there. Less than a block away, sitting outside this building, we found a hand truck stacked with boxes. The rope to hold them in was unhooked. While December kept an eye out for the delivery guy, I hoisted the top carton, read the label — "number of boxes — 1" — dumped it in beside Harley, and we moved out again.

"Where to?" December asked.

"Across the street. I can see the number from here."

"You're kidding?"

Somebody buzzed me in. I climbed two flights. A woman was waiting for me with the door ajar. The chain lock was still attached. Inside I could hear the television going. "Just leave it on the mat," the woman said and pushed money at me through the crack.

It was only a dollar.

"Told you," December said. "But it's a day's worth of bottles right there. And it only took five minutes." She banked it in the carrying case. "I saw the delivery boy and all he did was check his hair in a car mirror."

Next I did a two-box delivery from Romano's and got a dollar fifty from a man wearing dark glasses. Then I carried an Associated box full of cleaning stuff into a brownstone and a woman in a white uniform just thanked me and slammed the door.

"It's not fair," I told December. "That box weighed a ton." I could have ruptured something.

The next delivery we found was huge. "Number of boxes — 4." Two of them fit on the rack underneath the carriage and the other two had to go in with Harley.

"I can't see him anymore," December said.

The building was a lot of blocks away and 5B turned out to be a fourth-floor walk up. I was almost dead by the time I got the last box upstairs.

"That's it," I said to the lady. I could hardly talk. I felt like lying down right there in the hall.

"I know, I know." The lady was wearing a black and

green checked cap. She had a baby in her arms and another kid hiding behind her skirt. "It's a killer climb," she said. "I can't thank you enough."

Oh, brother, I thought. Not another thanker.

"Would you like a Coke?" the lady said.

She might try to get away with giving me a Coke instead of a tip. "Water," I said. The lady brought me a plastic glass with dinosaurs painted on it and a couple of warm cookies. She had rings on all her fingers.

"We just finished baking them, didn't we, sweet guys?" She smiled at her kids and then she handed me five dollars. "I hope you won't mind coming again," she said.

"Oh, no," I said. She was the nicest person yet.

On the way out, I slid down the last banister.

"All right!" I said to December. "That's more like it." Harley licked my hand and then my arm. I guess he liked sweat.

December opened the bank. "Watch my back. I'm going to count up. Seventeen fifty," she announced a moment later, "plus, wait a minute," she dug in her back pocket, "my ninety-five cents, your dollar, and the tokens. That's, let me see . . ."

". . . nineteen forty-five. I'm good at math. But I don't think you can buy things with tokens."

"That's a lot," said December.

"What did I tell you? Want a cookie? That lady gave me two."

December broke hers in half and inspected the inside. "No razor blades. I always check." She offered a piece to Harley, but he turned his head away. He was panting. "He's thirsty," December said. "I forgot about water."

"But where will we get it?" For a moment I thought about going back up and asking the nice lady.

"It's easy after a big rain. There are puddles. But it's got to be Satchel's street."

"Shouldn't we get the lipsticks first? Can't he get a drink at the park?"

"Satchel's is closer. Hang on, Harley. Water's coming."

We headed toward the river.

"There," December said finally. "You see? It's clean."

It was a short block of houses with little yards in front and flowers planted under all the trees. December unhooked Harley and put him down beside one of the rain puddles in the sidewalk. Harley lapped like mad.

"Does Satchel live here?" I asked.

"He did once. A long time ago. Before the rents went too high. Now he has no place. But still he comes back to sweep and wash down the sidewalk and stuff."

"Is it his job? Do they pay him?"

"I don't know. He says it will always be his street and he likes to watch flowers growing. That's enough, Harley. Back in the carriage."

Harley didn't want to go. He dug in his one front paw trying to hang on to the sidewalk.

"So, you want to keep going or what?" December asked.

"Don't you think we ought to buy the lipsticks and get them back to Annie?"

124 ·

"She's probably sleeping. She sleeps all afternoon on her bench," December said.

"Maybe we ought to check," I said. "I mean, how do you know she's there?"

"I know because I know. That's what she always does. Besides, we haven't got enough money yet. Half of it's yours, plus I already owe you and I owe Annie, so . . ."

"Wait," I said. "We're doing this for lipsticks. The other stuff can come later."

"Can we do it again tomorrow?"

"Sure. We'll even get a name, like a real business."

"Like what?"

"Well," I thought for a moment. "Like the Harley Gang or The Fast Food Company."

"I like The Fast Food Company," December said.

"Okay. We're The Fast Food Company. FF for code. That's how we'll talk about it when anyone's listening."

"I'm hungry," December said.

"There's that stuff from the diner wrapped in tinfoil," I said. "It's in the carrying case . . . I mean, the bank."

We sat in the sun on one of the stoops. The stuff in the bank turned out to be rice pudding. Maybe. We ate with our fingers. "After a while you get used to the taste," December said. Harley only sniffed it.

December peered into the bank. "There's always this grapefruit. But I hate grapefruit."

"So do I. I don't know why I brought it."

"Because it was big," December said.

I laughed. "So where do we buy the lipsticks?"

"A special drugstore." December balled up the tinfoil and stuck it back in the bank. "It has a whole makeup section and all the people wear white coats, like they're pretending they're doctors."

She let me push. Pushing was a lot more fun with Harley in the carriage. Sometimes the sidewalk was smooth enough to get up some speed. Finally December made me slow down. "It's that one, right up ahead."

I parked the carriage in front of the plate glass window. "They give me a hard time in this place," December said. "They're sure I'm going to swipe something. So I'm going to take fifteen dollars to show them, okay?" She brushed the front of her cords and straightened her cap.

"There's some . . ." I pointed, "dirt or something under your nose."

"I always get these stupid colds." December blew out her nose again and wiped her face with the sleeve of her jacket. "Okay?"

I nodded. Her nose was red, but it looked a little better.

Harley watched her go. The moment she disappeared through the door he started to whimper and whine and then, when she didn't come back, he lunged to the end of the safety straps and tried to throw himself out of the carriage.

I patted him. I talked to him. "It's okay. I'm here. Cut it out, Harley. She's buying lipsticks." I tried to get him interested in the grapefruit, tossing it like a ball and rolling it around in the carriage. Nothing worked. He began to howl.

An old man with a walker inched up beside me and stared into the carriage. "What are you doing to that dog?" he demanded. "Why is he all tied up?" The old man sucked at his teeth. "And what have you done to his leg?"

"It's not me," I said. "His owner's inside."

"Better be," the old man muttered. Then he shuffled off, stumping his walker.

"Shut up, Harley!" I tried to hold his jaws together, but he wriggled free, threw himself at the side of the carriage again, and went on howling. People stopped and stared. I wanted to strangle him. Instead I pretended to be looking for something in the store window. Humidifiers, hairbrushes, pink shower caps. What was taking December so long?

Finally I grabbed the handle of the carriage and took off down the street at a run. Harley was knocked off his legs. The surprise stopped him cold. So I raced him from one end of the block to the other. The wind blew Harley's ears backward.

The old man with the walker was waiting for the light to change. He glowered at me as I turned the carriage. "I knew it," he said.

When I roared back past the drugstore, December was on the steps looking around. I skidded to a stop and Harley pitched forward on his nose. "It was the only way to shut him up," I said.

"They had all the right colors," December said. "But they've changed the boxes. Now they're shiny black with gold lettering, so I only bought two. But I got a surprise. Nail polish with silver sparkles. It's really scintillating and it was on sale for a dollar ninety-nine, plus tax. Annie will love it."

Harley shook himself and licked his lips. He panted up at her. "Hey, Harley. Good dog," December said. She opened the bank.

"How much have we got left?" I asked.

"Wait. I'm counting. Six dollars and forty-eight cents, plus the tokens."

"So, is there anything else she wants?"

"I could pay her back and you, too. Or we could buy food. Annie loves food."

"Food," I said. "But I'm not staying with Harley anymore. He goes crazy. I get to buy this time."

We stopped at an A&P because December said they had the best bargains. "Annie's favorite is sweet things and her next favorite is black olives." December handed me four dollars. "I want to have some left."

Four dollars wasn't that much. It took me a long time to choose and then I had to go through the cash register line twice. The first time I didn't add up right and I had to put the little jar of grape jelly back. That's when I discovered the day-old food rack and so I had to put everything back, except the olives, and start all over again. The olives were a big problem. They cost a lot, even the small ones with the pits. And then, when I added it all up again, I had fifty-six cents left and I had to choose between potato chips and a can of Mighty Dog.

"I have one penny change from this stuff," I said to December, "and there are three coffees and extra creams and sugars in here."

December checked out the big bag. "Good on the olives, and candy corn, and marshmallows, great! We can toast them over my candle. And look, Harley, chicken and liver in a pop-top can for you."

"What's wrong with the doughnuts?" I asked.

"These are okay," December said, "but jelly's best."

"There weren't any jelly in the marked down section," I said.

December repacked everything in the bag. "I know Annie will like this. She won't even mind if we wake her up."

"I've been wondering about the bag of candy corn," I said on the way to the park. "It was marked down like three times. I'll bet they've had it since Halloween."

"I hope she likes the lipsticks," December said.

Kids were shouting in the playground. I could hear them even before we got to Cooper's. December pushed the carriage faster.

"She was wearing her blue coat last night," she said. "So we'll probably see her right away."

If she's there, I thought. I crossed my fingers.

16

The bench was empty. There was only Annie's cart with the broom parked in exactly the same spot.

The carriage slowed and then stopped.

Annie meant it, about going, I thought. And I've been busting my butt lugging those boxes around.

December began to push again, fast. Harley struggled to keep his balance.

When she reached the bench, December stared at it for a moment and then she checked the cart. The peach was still there on top of the black garbage bag. She turned it over in her hands like she was looking for bite marks.

I scanned the park. There were people on all the other benches again, but none of them was wearing a blue coat. The television man sat in front of his screen and the teeth lady was bent over, asleep, with her cheek resting on the concrete bench post. Her arms dangled down.

"My box, maybe," December said suddenly.

Harley whimpered from the carriage.

December came back across the cobblestones shaking her head. She sat on the edge of Annie's bench, with her hands between her knees. "I've got to think," she said.

Should I tell her about Annie saying "Get her off my neck"? It was mean that I knew and she didn't. But how did you tell a person something that hard?

"Go check the playground. Scope out the water fountain," December said.

Annie wasn't by the fountain. She wasn't at the picnic tables either.

In the sand playground kids were still digging with colored shovels and a mother was trying to pull a screaming little boy in a striped bathing suit off the slide. That's when I remembered about calling Mom.

Harley was sitting in December's lap when I got back. "Annie's not anywhere around," I said.

December pushed the visor of her baseball cap up and rubbed her forehead. "Now what am I going to do?"

"Can I borrow a quarter from the bank?" I asked. "I've got to call my mom."

"What can she do?"

"It's just that I forgot earlier."

There was a booth on the corner by Cooper's. But first I checked the tables outside under the sign, just in case, and then I looked through the window. But I didn't see Annie or Big Bucks or anybody.

No one answered at home. The phone at the diner rang and rang. It was the direct line to the kitchen. Finally someone picked up. *"Pronto, pronto."* It was Salvi. He didn't speak much English.

"Salvi. It's me, Sam," I shouted at him. "Get Flo."

"No Flo. Call back in the four o'clock," Salvi said.

"Thanks, Salvi." But he'd already hung up. I looked at my watch. It was 3:40. I leaned against the wall of the booth to rest my shoulders. If only Annie had waited, just a couple of hours more. Part of me wanted to stay in the phone booth until I could reach Mom, but I couldn't. Not with December back in the park.

The teeth lady woke up as I passed. "I know you." She lifted her head off the concrete post. "I've seen you. You're the one with the nice teeth."

"Oh, yeah," I said. "I remember."

"I've seen you," she repeated.

"Yeah," I said. "This morning."

I started to move away and then I thought maybe she'd seen Annie. "Have you seen the lady who lives on that bench over there?" I asked. "I mean, where my friend is sitting?"

"Sure. I've seen her. She has a blue coat." The lady nodded and smiled.

"That's her," I said. "When did you see her?"

"Lots of times."

"Today? Did you see her today?"

"Sure. I saw her. But I've got important work, you know. I'm busy." She began to paw through one of the shopping bags by the bench.

December was bent over on Annie's bench with her chin between Harley's ears.

"She's never not been here this long," she said.

"That woman says she saw her."

December looked over. "Oh, her. She sees everyone."

"That's what I thought," I said. Maybe I could tell December what Annie said, in pieces, like they tell people that someone is sick and getting sicker fast when all the time they're really dead. "So let's wait. I mean we have those coffees" — the end of the carriage was full of bags — "and all the food. . . ."

December's head lifted. "No. She's someplace and I've got to find her." She stood up and put Harley back in the carriage. He wagged his tail and sneezed when she snapped on the safety straps.

"I'll try the bagel place first, and then Trios. She goes there to wash. She told me about the bathroom, and the mints."

The bagel place was on Atlanta Boulevard. You could smell it before you got to it, a smell like onions and the elephant house at the zoo. "Not inside," December said. "Around the corner. That's where they dump the day-olds."

Next to the door into the kitchen was a huge metal bin on wheels. A man with one crutch was filling a shopping bag with bagels. The lid of the bin was padlocked shut, but one of the edges was bent up enough for him to get a hand inside. No way would I stick my hand down there in the dark, unless I was totally starving.

We walked to Trios without saying much. I kept hoping that any second, between the people on the sidewalk, I'd see a flash of blue and it would be Annie and I'd be wrong.

At Trios December checked the bathroom while I waited outside. Harley seemed to know something was up. He hardly howled at all.

When she came out, her mouth was set in that narrow line. "The guy yelled at me when I asked," she reported. "But I snagged a lot of napkins anyway." She blew her nose.

I looked around. We were close to the corner where Annie'd ambushed me yesterday. It was a real long shot, but there was a chance she might be there looking for me again.

December turned the carriage without asking why. The sun glinted off the mica in the sidewalk. Piles of garbage bags and junk waited by the curb.

Annie wasn't on the corner.

"This is so stupid," said December. "She never goes farther than Trios."

"She might," I said. "I mean, people change."

Harley had given up. He was lying on his side, his eyes half shut. I didn't blame him. My feet were hot inside my sneakers. I wished I could go straight home and turn on the air conditioner and get a huge glass of OJ from the refrigerator and lie on the sofa and watch the first thing that came on TV. Or maybe just go to sleep.

December stared at the bank across the street. There

was a woman by the cash machine with her hand out, begging for money. "That's it," she said suddenly. "I forgot."

"Forgot what?"

"She's collecting money. She doesn't know I've already got some. I'm going back to the park to wait."

"But has she done that before?"

"What's wrong with it? How else could she buy lipsticks when she's sad and getting doomed?"

I'd never thought about Annie and money, but money made sense. It really did. I ran to catch up.

"I mean, for this long?" I said. "Without her cart?"

" 'Course. Nobody touches her cart. I already told you."

December tore along, maneuvering the carriage around and between people heading home from work. Everyone seemed to be going the other way except for this one weirdo carrying a big green-and-white flowered armchair on his head. It looked so funny — four wooden legs sticking up and two legs walking underneath. December wheeled past him but I snuck a look. It was July.

"Hey! July! It's July," I said to December, but she didn't stop. I grabbed the handle of the carriage.

"Yo, Sam." July turned half around, slowly, like he had a stiff neck. "What did I tell you about Thursdays?" He grinned. "Best day for mungo picking."

"You mean you found it?" I asked. Next to me I could hear December snuffing through her nose.

"Yup. A genuine antique wing chair. Springs aren't even busted." He patted one of the arms. "Carriage looks real sharp. How's the dog liking it?"

"He's the one I told you about," I said. December shot me a furious glance.

"But you didn't tell me he was part Jack Russell." July started walking again. I kept a hand on the carriage. "He's got to be with those ears and that handle of a tail."

"Is that good?" I asked.

"Samson!" December hissed at me.

"The best," July said. "I had three Jack Russells back in Kentucky." He eased his head around to look at December. "Bet this guy is a good ratter."

"It's been nice meeting you," December said.

"But what happened to your leg, little fellow?" July said to Harley. "A fight? I know how you Jack Russells like to argue."

Harley stared up at him as if he understood every word.

"Yeah," I said. "His leg's sort of mashed."

"Well, bring him around tomorrow when I have my hands free," July said. "I know a bit about dogs." He stopped at the corner. "So long, little fellow." He smiled at December. "See you, Sam."

"One night Harley killed two rats," December said suddenly. "So fast."

Harley sat very straight in the carriage like a wounded hero.

July nodded. "Like I said, best ratters in the world."

The light changed. He strolled across the street as if carrying a chair on your head was the only way to go.

"Who is he?" December bumped the carriage over the next curb.

"July. Remember, I told you about him and his mother."

"The super? Then he's the man I heard in the basement."

"He's nice," I said. "I talk to him a lot."

"What did you tell him? Did you tell him about me?"

"No. Only about Harley. Promise."

A block later December said, "Annie's going to really like the olives. They'll make her happy. You'll see."

If she's back, I thought. If December was right about the money.

"And then we'll have the food," December went on, "and give her the lipsticks and the sparkly polish."

"The coffees are sort of old." I wondered how much Annie could make in a day, begging.

"She won't mind," December said.

But when we got to the park, even before we were under the trees, I saw Satchel standing by Annie's bench. And I saw the blue coat. Annie's coat. Satchel clutched it with both hands in front of his chest. It was worse than seeing the empty bench, worse than not seeing the coat at all.

17
....

Satchel stood without moving, just waiting for us to reach him. I didn't want to look at him or the blue coat, and I didn't want to look at December. I watched my sneakers walking across the cobblestones until right at the edge of where I was looking were the wheels of Annie's cart.

"What are you doing with that coat?" December said. "Where did you get it?"

Satchel cleared his throat. "It's for you, little lady. Annie says."

"I don't want it." December sounded really angry. "Where is she, anyway?"

The coat sort of hung there between them.

"She's gone home," Satchel said.

I heard a sound from December like she'd been socked in the stomach. It was awful, but I felt relieved. At least now she knew.

"What home? She hasn't got any home," she said. "Her home's all burned up."

"Well, I don't know about that," Satchel said. "I guess I'll just rest her coat here on the bench. Won't be in anyone's way."

"So, when's she coming back?" December demanded.

"I don't know," said Satchel. "She's gone south. But Annie says to tell you about the morning and looking ahead. . . . Oh, my, that's not how it went, I have it here, just like she told it. She wrote the words down." He reached into the pocket of the blue coat and pulled out a folded piece of paper.

"I don't want that," December said.

Satchel stood with the scrap of paper in his hand. His eyes looked so sad that finally I took it. "She gave me a raisin bagel, last thing," he said to me. "Not too hard. I wet it up good in the water fountain and it went down real easy." He was edging away. "She was some fine woman," he added. "Her and her jokes. She could surely make a body laugh." He cleared his throat again. "So, little lady, I'll be seeing you."

I could hear December breathing, short breaths, close together. This was what Annie meant, I thought. This was the bad time. December bent over the carriage and unstrapped Harley's harness and picked him up in her arms. Then she sat down on the bench as far away from the coat as she could get, and rocked back and forth. Harley began to lick her face all over.

I know it sounds stupid, but all I could think about were the new lipsticks. I wondered if we could return them and the nail polish and get our money back. You know how sometimes a dumb thought gets a hold of you and it's like you're stuck with it. But if December was going to return them, I figured it should be right away, quick, while the guy at the store still remembered her. She could show him that the black boxes hadn't even been opened.

And maybe I could take the candy corn and the olives back, too. No one I knew liked olives. But I didn't know whether to say any of that to December.

December coughed and blew her nose on a napkin. "Get Harley's water dish, will you," she said. "It's right in the top of my pack."

"What should I do with this note?" I asked.

"I don't care." She almost grabbed the angel box out of my hand and then she marched off with Harley toward the playground.

As soon as she was gone I unfolded the note. I don't know why. I thought maybe it might say where Annie was or tell us what to do or something. But it looked like a poem, not a letter. There were only a few lines written in pencil and no dear anybody and no name at the bottom.

"There is a way. There is a place. You are she that looketh forth as the morning, fair as the moon, clear as the sun. Believe it."

I read it again, twice. And then I was sorry. It wasn't for me. It was private.

December came back slowly, holding Harley and

balancing the angel dish full of water. I stuffed the note into my pocket. I'll save it, I thought. And give it to her sometime.

"I'm going to wash his leg now," December said, "and then I'm going to use the other half of my pink T-shirt for a new bandage. This one's probably infected. Then I'll decide."

What time was it? I was standing in tree shadow, but it was still bright sunlight on the street. 6:40. I had to call Mom before she got frantic. I opened the bank and took another quarter. "I'll be right back," I said.

The phone at the diner was picked up on the first ring, but all I heard was the clang of pots and then in the distance shouts and cheering. "Salvi?" I yelled. "Salvi?" Maybe I had the wrong number.

"Pronto, pronto."

"Salvi? It's Sam. Get Flo."

"Hold up, hold up," shouted Salvi.

I heard him yelling for Mom and then Manny was on the line. "You're missing all the fun," he said.

"What's happening? Where's Mom?"

"Get your butt over here. On the double. Take a taxi."

Somebody tooted a party horn into the phone.

"What's the big rush?"

"Big money!" Manny said. "Your ma's won the lottery!"

*   *   *

December was holed up in the box when I got back. The

carriage and Annie's cart were parked outside like a barricade and inside she'd put the red rug down again. The cardboard still felt cold and clammy.

"So come with me," I said as soon as I told her about Mom winning the lottery.

"Why should I?"

"Because we're rich. Rich! Don't you get it? It's going to change everything."

"For you, maybe." December wrapped a strip of pink T-shirt around Harley's leg. "I'm tired and they wouldn't let Harley in anyway."

"Maybe they would, now." Rich! I kept thinking it and saying it, waiting for it to seem real.

December gave me a funny look. "If you're so rich, I bet you won't want to do the business anymore. I bet you'll forget all about the FF. I bet you won't ever come back."

"I will so. I'll take a taxi, both ways."

"Taxis aren't so great," December said. "I had to take a lot of them one night. When they couldn't find a place for me to sleep."

I didn't want to leave her there. "Come on," I said. "Mom really liked you. She told me."

December coughed and blew her nose again. "No. I'm staying here with Harley."

For some reason, I didn't want to go without her. "Please," I said. "We can hide him like before."

"No. But bring me some of those little hot dog things," December said. "For Harley. And some new coffee."

"Okay. But don't go anywhere," I said. What was it

that was making me feel so creepy? "I'll be right back."

"I've still got your socks," December said.

I sprinted to the corner. There were taxis with their signs lit up everywhere, but none of them would stop. They don't for kids. I had to wait until one pulled up at a red light and then I jumped in before he could lock the doors.

"Just my luck," the driver said.

"Atlanta Boulevard and Twenty-ninth," I told him.

"You sure you got the money?"

"Sure."

The driver eyed me through the mirror. He doesn't think I do, I thought. He doesn't have a clue about Mom. I could probably buy this taxi. I could buy the whole fleet. To deliver groceries. But hey! I wouldn't need to — and neither would December. Because I'd ask Mom, first thing, to get a bigger apartment. Big enough for me and Mom and December and Harley.

I felt like yelling out the window.

And Tommy and Lou, wait till I told them. I'd buy tickets to all the Sox games. Maybe even a box right behind the dugout so I could get autographs.

I thought of telling the driver that my mom was a millionaire. But then he'd expect a big tip, and I didn't have any money yet. What would I say to him if Mom wasn't waiting outside?

Mom wasn't, but Manny was. He had a party horn stuck through the hole in his ear.

He handed the driver a five. "Keep the change," he said like they do on TV.

"Gee, thanks," the driver said.

"Don't thank me. It's his ma's money." Manny draped an arm across my shoulders. "Come on, kid. She's waiting."

The diner was wild. Everyone was out in the aisles or leaning over the back of the booths talking to everyone else. Mona came through the swinging doors from the kitchen holding a tray over her head. "Listen up, you guys," she yelled. "Dessert's on me!"

"Oh, Sam!" Mom threw her arms around my neck. "We won the lottery." She was laughing and crying at the same time. "It's a miracle. And the chicken bones did it . . ."

"What chicken bones?"

"The ones in the drawer. Your dream!"

Manny clapped me on the back.

"It won!" Mom jumped up and down and pulled on my hands. "For me and Mona."

"Mona?" I said.

"So," Manny said. "You going to lend me some money?"

The people in the booth next to me applauded and broke into "For she's a jolly good fellow."

Mona grabbed me from the other side and planted this big gooey kiss on my cheek. "Hey, dream boat," she said. "Thanks to you, my ship has come in."

"Where's that free dessert?" someone yelled.

"Well, excuse my shoes," Mona said.

Salvi brushed by, carrying another tray. "¡Felicidades!" He beamed at me.

Mom spit on a corner of her apron and scrubbed at my cheek. "Lipstick," she said.

"So, my birthday's next month," Manny said. "I could use a new earring."

"Let's go to the back booth," Mom said. "Where it's quieter."

Salvi brought us pieces of Death by Chocolate Cake and two Cokes. "Sssh, Cokes freebees," he whispered.

Mom told me the whole story, about how Mona had found out on her break and come shrieking back to the diner and no one had been able to understand a word she was saying. "She's going to Seattle," Mom said. "For good. She says it's always cool in Seattle."

"When? How soon?"

"Next week. She says she's going to start over out there."

Great! Then December could move in right away, I thought, even before we found the big apartment.

"But what are we going to do, Mom?"

"Start a college fund," Mom said instantly. "That was always your dad's dream for you and Beans. I only wish they were here to see this day." She wiped her eyes with her lacy handkerchief and stuffed it back in her vest pocket.

"Yeah. But what else?" I said.

"Go away for the weekend sometime. To the seashore or the mountains. Get tickets to a musical show. I always wanted to see one of those."

"But what about a new apartment? A big one. With a bedroom for you and everything."

"Oh, hon." Mom laughed. "It's not *that* much."

"What do you mean?" I stared at her. "Manny said . . ."

"Twenty-eight thousand dollars," Mom said. "Fourteen thousand for Mona and fourteen thousand for me. And I figure if I put it all in a savings account right away it will be enough to see you through four years of college."

"Is that all?" That wasn't big money. That wasn't even rich and I'd told December we were millionaires.

Mom was crying again. "That's plenty," she said. "What more do we need?"

I slumped back in the seat. Nothing was solved. Everything was exactly the same. Except I felt worse than before, like I'd been dropped on my head.

Mom was still crying and smiling at me across the table. I tried to smile back, but inside I was thinking that this was worse than the coat, worse than Annie's leaving.

"I'm really glad about the lottery," I said to Mom. "But I've got to go now." Lucky I hadn't told December about the big apartment.

"What about supper?"

"I'm not hungry. But can I have a double order of pigs-in-blankets?" I asked. "To go. And some hot coffee?"

"Sam, where are you?" Manny bellowed. He came down the aisle. "Phone's for you. By the cash register."

"Me?"

"If it's Lou," Mom said, "want to ask him to a baseball game? My treat."

"It's a gal," Manny winked at Mom. "Watch out, Flo. They'll all be after him now."

Girl? I didn't know any girls. The receiver was lying on the counter, but when I picked it up there was no one on the line. Just a dial tone.

"Gimme a break," I said.

"What?" Manny said. "She hang up on you?"

"Ha, ha. Not funny." I was teed-off at him already. Him and his big money.

"There *was* a gal there. No kidding. Sounded anxious to talk to you, too."

"Yeah, sure."

Manny shrugged. "Maybe it wasn't for you. She asked for Samson, but she could have meant Salvi. Never mind." He punched my arm. "They always call back."

Samson! It had to be December. How had she gotten the number? "Wait a minute. What did she say again?" I asked.

Manny opened the cash register and began to make change for a customer. "She said, 'Is this the City Lights Diner?' and then she said, 'I need to speak to Samson. Quick. It's important.'" Manny leered at me. "And I said, 'Okay, babe, I'll get him.' That's it. Word for word." He slammed the cash register drawer shut.

Important. What was so important? Important could mean that Annie was back, but she wouldn't have called me for that. Suddenly this little shiver ran up between my shoulder blades.

Mom was in the kitchen. I stuck my head through the swinging doors. "Hey, Mom, I got to go. Now."

"Wait. I'm just packing your pigs. All I need are the mustards."

"Forget it," I said. "I'll take them raw."

When I reached the street, I remembered I didn't have any money. Forget a taxi, I couldn't even take a bus.

So I ran. And stopped to rest. And ran again. Maybe it was Harley. Maybe something had happened to him. Half way there, I heard sirens coming up behind me. Two police cars, their blue lights flashing, wailed past me. And after them a fire engine. Not the park, I prayed, not the park, not the park. Don't make this the bad time Annie was talking about. Please.

18

A whole string of police cars was already there, parked every which way. And a fire engine with firemen dragging at the hose. And a crowd of people. And two ambulances. Black smoke billowed up into the branches of the trees. Lights jittered and blinked.

Then I saw the white van parked up on the sidewalk next to the chain link fence. My heart hammered in my ears.

I skirted the edge of the crowd, but I couldn't see over peoples' heads, so I wiggled my way to the front. The police were holding the crowd back. "Fire's out. Keep moving. Go on home. Party's over."

The trash cans were still smoking and all the benches were empty. I looked beyond them for December's box. The carriage and Annie's cart were there and so was the box, but it was all smashed in. I wanted to yell for December, but I didn't dare, and the police weren't letting anyone through.

Two men in white coats carried a stretcher with someone on it right by me to the open door of the ambulance. I didn't see the face. All I saw was a shoe. And a yellow sock. Big Bucks.

The crowd shifted. "Is he dead?" "I don't know." There were voices all around me. "I heard it was clubs." "I thought it was a fire." "Yeah. A couple of guys with baseball bats on a rampage." "But that's crazy!"

Then I saw the teeth lady. She was sitting on the ground with her back against a tree just a few feet away. A woman got out of the white van with a blanket and came over to her. Suddenly the streetlights blinked on.

The police weren't guarding December's end of the park anymore. I squeezed back through the crowd and edged around behind. No one paid any attention to me. When I reached the shadow of the building, I checked for cops again and then I slipped along the wall, dropped to my hands and knees, and crawled between the carriage and Annie's cart.

The box was ruined. Only my red rug was left, scrunched in a corner. I knelt just inside the entrance, trying to think. Maybe the white van people had her. Maybe the guys with the bats had beaten her up and she was already in the ambulance with Big Bucks. Maybe she was dead.

I wondered if I would sense it if she were, like Mom did. She'd been in the shower when it happened, washing her hair, and she said she stopped all of a sudden with her arms over her head and couldn't move. Later the police told her that was almost exactly the time Dad and Beans were killed. Mom said her hair was still wet when they came.

I crouched as still as I could, waiting to feel something, but all I felt was me, scared. Then I got a message. Harley. If December were dead or taken, Harley would be hobbling around the park howling his head off. And Harley wasn't there. So they had to be together, somewhere.

But where?

Outside I heard sirens fading into the distance.

I backed out of the box and peered over the top. The crowd had thinned to a few people and the ambulances and the white van were gone. I saw the flashing blue lights of the last police car as it eased into the traffic.

One corner of the box was blackened and the top was split open. I felt the gash with my fingers. It went all the way through. Those guys weren't kidding, I thought. If I'd been in the box . . . that's when I saw the writing on the cardboard. Just one word, "pear," in her script with a lot of loopy lines underneath.

Pear?

P-e-a-r. Fruit? That didn't make any sense. I stared at the lines. It looked like a kid's drawing of waves. Or water. Water! That was it. Those lines meant water.

The grocery bags were still in the carriage, but her backpack was gone. She must be lugging Harley. I decided to take the carriage.

The sun hung behind the buildings, half a giant ball in a haze of bright yellow. It helped to be out of the silent, empty park and on the street with people and lighted shop windows. Noise and food smells from the restaurants spilled onto the sidewalk.

Just before I reached Trios I cut west toward the river. The sun was down. Stringy gray clouds trailed across the pinky sky. It was hard to keep jogging with the carriage, and I thought about dumping it. Finally the buildings ended. I rolled the carriage back and forth while I waited for the light. Then I crossed Shore Line Drive and bumped onto the boards of the wooden pier. It stretched away in front of me, flatter and darker than the river. Halfway out on one of the railing beams I saw her, silhouetted against the silvery water. I almost cried. I was so scared she wouldn't be there.

Harley went into a frenzy of barking.

"It's okay, Harley. It's only me."

I could hear waves slapping against the pilings under my feet. Was she hurt?

"Hey, December. I got your message."

Behind her, lights moved on the water and there were more lights on the far shore.

"I spelled pier wrong," December said. Her voice sounded funny, hoarse like she'd been crying, but it was too dark to see her face. "I spelled it like fear." Harley whimpered and sneezed.

"That's okay," I said. "I got here anyway."

"I knew it wasn't right, but I didn't have time. I was scared they'd come back."

"Are you . . . did they get you?" I asked.

"Almost. They hit at everyone."

"Why?"

"I don't want to talk about it. They just did."

"I saw Big Bucks," I said. "On a stretcher."

"I don't want to know."

"They took him to the hospital."

"I hid in the box," December said. "And then they set it on fire. But it wouldn't burn — it was still too soggy. Harley wanted to get at them. He tried to bark, so I bundled his head all up in the rug."

"Good old Harley." I sat down next to December on the beam. She was shivering. Harley stretched his head toward me and sniffed at my arm. I scratched his ears.

"He's really hungry," December said. "Did you bring the pigs?"

I looked down at my hands. "I had them," I said. "And some coffee too. I swear. I must have dropped them." I couldn't remember them at all. "And we're not rich either. It wasn't what I thought."

"I don't care," said December. "But I need something for Harley to eat."

"There's dog food in the carriage," I said. "And olives."

December scrubbed at her face with the sleeve of her jacket. "What happened to the marshmallows?"

Suddenly I felt better, sort of goofy. I started to laugh. "The Fast Food Company has everything," I said.

Harley ate right out of the can. I could hear him slurping in the dark. "When he's had enough, we'd better go," I said.

"Go where?"

"Back. It's too dark out here."

"No," December said. "I'm not going back there ever."

"I don't mean the park," I said.

"And I'm not going back to your house, either."

"Who said anything about my house?" I picked up Harley and put him in the carriage.

"I like it here." December trailed after me. "And I'm not going any more places with weirdos I don't even know." She grabbed for the handle.

I swerved the carriage away from her.

"Listen you," December shouted. "Wherever it is, I don't want to go."

I kept pushing.

"You're such a knownothing jerk sometimes. . . !"

I didn't answer.

"Don't wheel so fast," December said. "Harley can't balance." Then she shut up.

But she started in again when we reached my street. "I knew it. I knew we were going here. And I told you, no! I don't want your old mother. I've had too many mothers. So stop! Give me that carriage!"

I swung the carriage around and began to bump it backward up the stoop steps. December hung on to the front. The bag of groceries tipped over. "Watch your leg, Harley," I said. I got the carriage to the front door, but then December dug in her feet and hauled. She was really strong. If I'd let go without any warning she would have fallen down the steps with the carriage on top of her.

So I kept a hold of it while I lifted Harley out. Then I

said, "Okay, take it, if you want it so much," and then I let go.

Now that December had the carriage, she just stood there like she didn't know what to do with it. I unlocked the front door. "Come on, Harley. In here," I said.

"Hey! You can't take my dog." December pushed in behind me before the door latched and grabbed at my arm. "I thought you were my friend." Friend came out funny. She was crying.

"You can have him back," I said. "In about a minute."

The elevator was there, but still I had to stand listening to her snuffling the whole way down. "Oh, boy," she whispered. "Oh, boy. You've had it."

July's desk lamp was off. Only the bare bulb hanging from the ceiling was on. December stayed by the elevator. "One minute," she said. "I'm giving you one minute."

A strip of light showed under July's door. Before I could knock, it opened and July filled the doorway.

"Sam? What's up?" He tucked a short-sleeved shirt into his work pants. Behind him I could hear the announcers doing the Sox game.

"Remember what you said about Thursdays? About them being the best day for mungo picking?"

"Sure do." July rubbed the top of his head.

"Well," I said. "It's still Thursday."

19
. . . .

"So what did you find that couldn't wait till morning?" July said.

"Actually two things," I said.

July raised an eyebrow.

"It's Harley, here," I went on. "And her." December hadn't moved. She stood beside the elevator, her hands flat against the wall.

"I see," July said.

I took a deep breath. "There was this woman in the park," I said, "but she's gone and now these guys with baseball bats are bashing people and setting fires and . . ."

"Whoa." July held up a hand. "Hold on a minute." He disappeared into his room. I could feel December glaring. "That's another minute," she said.

The television went off and then July came back with an old wicker rocker. He set it next to the green and

156 ·

white armchair and then he went around behind his desk. He had to pass right by December, but he acted like he didn't see her.

"First let me take a look at the dog," he said.

"He wants to look at Harley," I said to December.

"Put him right there on the blotter." July cleared some papers away. He fiddled with the gooseneck lamp until the light shone on Harley's back.

"It's okay, Harley," I said.

"It's hard to make a sling for a dog." July ran his hands along Harley's sides, parting the hairs and peering at the bald spots. "You did a good job of wrapping."

"It wasn't me. It was her."

I heard a sound from December. She took a step away from the wall.

July began to undo the strips of T-shirt. Harley sat with his head bent, following every movement with his eyes.

The place on his leg was red and gooey. To me it looked worse than before, but July's face showed only interest, the same look he'd had when we were fixing the carriage. "What do you think?" I asked.

"These bald places are hot spots. No problem. They'll clear up on their own once we're into cooler weather."

"He's my dog," December said suddenly. "And I already got told that."

"Good," said July. "But this here leg is a horse of a different color."

"I know that," said December. "I'm planning to take him to a real vet tomorrow."

"A vet's a good idea," said July. "This looks like a case of moist eczema."

December took a step toward the desk. "Is that bad?"

"No worse than a road burn," July said. "What this little fellow needs is a few good soakings in a Domeboro solution, but that'll have to wait till the drugstore opens. In the meantime I'd like to apply some cortisone ointment and rebandage his leg." He looked at December. "If that meets with your approval."

December stared at him from under the brim of her cap.

"He knows a lot about fixing things," I said.

July rested a hand on Harley's back. He didn't seem to care how long December took to make up her mind. Finally she gave a little nod. "He really needs water," she said.

July tilted the shade of the lamp so it wasn't shining in Harley's eyes. "Watch he doesn't jump off the desk."

While he was gone, I held on to Harley in case December grabbed him and tried to make a run for it. A moth fluttered around the light. It was so quiet in the basement I could hear its wings beating.

July came back with a tube of ointment and a bowl of water. He put the bowl on the desk under Harley's nose and showed December the tube. "It's an antiinflammatory," he said, "and it won't sting. It'll just feel cool to him. But you should put it on. He trusts you."

July readjusted the light and Harley held up his leg as if he knew what he should do. December edged up to the desk. "Hold out your hand," July told her and then he squeezed a long curl of white stuff onto her stiff fingers. All the time I kept a grip on Harley's rear end. "Slather it on," July said. "Don't be shy." Harley licked December's wrist.

"Okay," July said finally. "That should do. Now wrap him up again. You're the expert."

When December was through, she lifted Harley into her arms. I wanted to hang on to his tail, but it seemed too stupid.

"Well, the patient looks raring to go," July said, "but I think the rest of us should sit down." He lowered himself into his swivel chair. I moved over to the wicker rocker. It was closer to the elevator in case December tried to split. Finally she sat on the very edge of the green and white armchair.

"Okay," July said. "Somebody want to fill me in on the details?"

December hunched farther over Harley. So I told him. About Annie and the park and Big Bucks and the foster families. Any minute I was sure December was going to kill me, but I couldn't stop talking. I told him about the "Rebecca" woman and the white van and all the searching and the refrigerator box and the guys with the bats. And then I told him about Mom's lottery. At that, both of July's eyebrows lifted.

"I thought the money was going to fix it," I said. "But it wasn't such a big deal. It's only good enough for college. So I need a place, I mean she and Harley need a place, to stay. For a little while. Until I can figure something else." That was it. I'd run out. "I thought maybe she could stay in the back room. There's a place there, behind the bureau."

December stiffened. "Don't," she said.

I looked at July. "She's stayed there before."

"I know," July said.

The stupid moth banged its head against the lamp-shade.

"You do?" said December.

"Yup. I've owned this building for a long time," July said. "And you might say it talks to me."

December turned on me. "You told me he was the super."

"That, too," said July. "I'm a little bit of everything."

"But you didn't say anything? Didn't you wonder?" I asked.

"I thought about it," July said. "But by the time I was through thinking, there was no one back there."

"That's when I came down to ask about an air conditioner," I said. "I found her and Harley and took them upstairs for food."

"I figured as much," July said.

"So can she stay?" I asked. "She can pay. I mean, we've got a job and all."

"The carriage!" December said. "I left it out there. I have to get it."

I jumped up. "I'll go."

"Sit down, Sam," said July.

"No, really. Let me do it. It's better."

"Sit down!" July said again. It wasn't a suggestion. So I sat and watched December press the elevator button and get in with Harley in her arms. The elevator doors closed on both of them.

Suddenly I felt so tired, really beaten, like I'd tried my best move and all I needed was a little help and July had let me down.

"You don't understand." There was no point anymore in explaining, but I said it anyway. "Now she's got the dog. She'll split."

"Maybe so," July said. "Maybe so. But you couldn't hang on to that dog forever."

He leaned back in his swivel chair and put his feet on the desk, like he didn't care.

I watched the moth, so dogged and so dumb. Give up, I thought, just give up.

"Funny," July said. "I always thought I was the champion mungo picker."

I pictured December bumping the carriage down the stoop. And Harley in his safety harness. I wondered where she'd head to. The pier maybe, or Satchel's street. No, I thought, it'll be some doorway somewhere with the carriage to barricade her and Harley to guard against the rats.

The moth found a way under the lampshade and butted at the bulb, still trying to get at the light. I wondered how long it would be before I stopped looking for her.

20
. . . .

Then I heard the elevator creaking down. The doors opened and the carriage nosed out. It really was the carriage with Harley in it and December behind, pushing. I couldn't believe it. I was so sure I was never going to see her again. It was like looking at her brand new.

I began to rock like crazy. December wheeled the carriage into the light. July put his feet down and stood up.

"Well, hello again," he said to Harley. Then he turned to December. "I don't believe I know your name. Mine's July Sixteenth Simms." He held out his hand.

December stared up at him.

"Mine's December First," she said. "And this is Harley Davidson."

"December First?" said July. He shook her hand. "Well, I'll be . . ."

"But that's not my born name," December said. "That's my now name."

"So can she stay?" I burst out. "In the back room? Behind the bureau?"

"Just until the drugstore opens," December said.

"December First." July kept shaking his head.

"Well, can she?"

"No." July let go of December's hand. "Not behind the bureau," he said. "We can do better than that for a December First. Sounds to me she's kin."

The first thing July did was turn on the overhead lights and open the heavy wooden shutters over the windows in the back room. Then he sent me to get a bucket of water and a mop and some clean rags. When Harley saw July roll in the big industrial vacuum cleaner, he bristled and went on the attack. December put him down and he planted himself in front of the machine and barked his head off.

"Good dog," July said. "Keep an eye on it, while I get my toolbox."

"Where do you want to be?" I asked December.

She pointed to the corner where I'd found her hiding.

When July came back I helped him moved things until we'd cleared a space about the size of my bedroom. December dumped the old rags into a garbage bag and July mopped the floor, even though it looked perfectly clean to me. I had to vacuum everywhere, including the walls.

"I'd better call and tell Mom where I am," I said when I was through.

"Use the phone on my desk," July said.

It took a long time. First I had to get past Salvi, and

then Mom had to go through the lottery business again. July passed me a couple of times carrying things.

When I got back, a wooden bed was already set up with a headboard and a mattress and blankets and everything. July and December pushed the bed into the corner. Then July moved the bureau until it jutted out like a kind of half wall with the drawers facing in.

"You two poke around," he said. "See what else you can find. I'm going to wash the windows."

"It's pitch dark outside," I said.

"For the sun," July said. "In the morning."

December followed me to the lumber room with Harley limping along behind. I found a good chair and then I spotted something even better. "What about this bookcase?"

"All the shelves sag in the middle," December said.

"We can flip them over."

I dragged it to the back room and set it up like another half wall at the foot of the bed.

"Wait," I said. "I've got a great idea." I hauled the box of *National Geographics* from the general junk room.

"I've got my own books," December said.

"But these are heavy. They'll flatten out the shelves. And they have great pictures of volcanoes and countries like Australia and Mexico."

I sat down on the floor and began to flip through pages. Harley put his good paw on the edge of the box and peered in. After a moment December sat down next to me.

"See? Here's a really cool picture of a flood."

"Hey, Sam." July stood in the doorway. "Take over for me out here, will you? My arms are too big to fit through the bars."

He handed me a wad of newspaper and a spray bottle of cleaner.

The windows were covered with scrolly iron gates and it was hard to reach through them. But it was nice to be outside where even in the dark you could see sky and the outline of trees leaning over the fence. As if it were a backyard in the country. The dead palm tree from 3B was in its pot right outside the door.

I started in with the newspapers. For a while it seemed as if I was only making the windows worse. The ammonia stuff just smeared the gunk around. Then, like magic, the film of dirt disappeared and I could see into the back room clear as anything. December leafed through the last *National Geographic* and put it on a shelf. Harley sniffed the box and I saw July carrying that old wicker elephant table and a lamp.

"Now, all I got to do is dig up a towel and a footstool," I heard him say, "so you can reach the faucets on that big sink in the utility room. That'll do for starters." He turned on the lamp and picked up the empty *National Geographics* box. "How're you coming with those windows?" he called to me.

"I'm almost done." I crumpled up another sheet of newspaper.

July came out into the yard. For a while he stood without saying anything. Then, "I want you to bring your mother in on this, Sam," he said. "So the four of us can sit down tomorrow."

"But it's all set, isn't it?"

"I wish it were," July said. "But there's a lot of thinking to do yet, and a lot of hurdles to get over."

"She can't go back to that park," I said.

"I'm not saying she has to," July said. "All I'm saying is it won't be easy. But we'll find a way."

A way. Annie had said that, too. There is a way. There is a place.

"Lock up when you're through out here," July said. He stopped at the door before going in and looked at the palm tree. "Well, what do you know. A new green shoot already."

On his way out of the back room July switched off the overhead light. "I'll leave the one on in the hall," he said to December.

For a long time December just stood in the middle of the little lighted room. Then she shrugged out of her backpack and put it on the chair. Great, I thought, she's going to unpack her stuff, but all she took out was the Mickey Mouse. I could see his little white glove waving. She held him by his red shorts and began to walk slowly around the room. She showed Mickey the bookcase and the chair and the bureau and even under the bed. Finally she stood him on the elephant table right beside the lamp.

Then she picked up Harley and sat down on the bed. He crawled out of her lap and headed straight for the pillow. He smelled it all over and scratched at the pillowcase with his good paw. He sneezed. Then he turned around and around and around until at last he settled down in the hollow he had made.

Suddenly I felt happy the way I did sometimes when I was walking at night on the street and I got a glimpse into a lighted window and saw people living there, all safe.

I knocked on the glass. December looked startled. Then she got off the bed and came out into the yard.

"Look at Harley," I said. "All curled up."

December stared through the window. "It's nice," she said. "I guess he's never slept on a pillow before."

"And you can let him outside whenever you feel like it."

"I have to go back to the park tomorrow," December said after a moment. "First thing."

"No! Why?"

"To get Annie's cart. In case."

There was no in case. Annie was gone. As gone as Dad and Beans. Her good-bye note was in my pocket. But all I said was, "Okay. If you have to." Maybe I'd give the note to December later, after the park, or even the day after that. She could keep it and read it whenever she felt like it. It wasn't as good as having Dad's watch, but it was something. "I'll go with you," I said.

December sighed. She took off her baseball cap and ran her fingers through her funny white hair.

"I'll bet you don't know what Samson means?" she said.

"Scintillating?"

"No. Annie told me it means Lord of the Sun."

Lord of the Sun. Moon Queen. That sounded like Annie.

The light from the window shone on December's hair.

Maybe Annie wasn't so crazy after all. Believe it, the note said. Maybe Annie was right. Maybe that was what you had to do.